The Fairies of Carlow:

The Outsider

Book Two

By Sonja Danielson

Follow Sonja Danielson on:

Pinterest @sonjadanielson

Facebook @sonjadanielson

www.sonjadanielson.com

She would love to hear from you:

Sonjadanielson@gmail.com

I dedicate this book (again!) with love to my husband and family, who continue to amaze me with their support and love. Also, I send deepest thanks to my high school English teacher, Connie Henshaw, who taught me that creative writing is important. You were a true blessing to a shy and dorky teenager.

Table of Contents

Chapter One

The polished marble floor tilted precariously under her feet as Princess Morgen stared at her father in horror. He may be the king of the fairy kingdom of Meath, and reckless with his power, but she could not imagine even he would go this far. "You cannot mean this."

He slouched on his ornate throne with his arms akimbo over the deeply carved armrests. His beard lay on his chest in an unkempt, wiry mass. Morgen, on the other hand, stood straight and tall before him, her hair neat and tidy in the traditional woven braids of her kingdom, and her gown brushed and well-fitted. Grim and disapproving courtiers surrounded her as they filled the cavernous throne room. They were not displeased with the king, however. They did not want to share a room, no matter how massive, with her. She did her best to ignore them and focus her attention on her father. His eyes narrowed at her show of defiance. "I mean every word."

"But, Carlow?" She sputtered the words of the hated kingdom. "They are barbarians. Worse than sprites. Why would you send me there?"

His expression hardened and he jerked his body forward. Even before this room full of witnesses, he would not hesitate to treat her harshly. "It is not your place to question my authority." His booming voice rattled the crystalline ornaments hanging from the wall sconces. They were shaped like tear drops, which matched Morgen's emotions, yet she would not cry in front of this man. He may be her father, but that was in name only. He was her monarch and nothing more. No. He was her tormentor as well, but she refused to give him the satisfaction of breaking her. Determined not to show her vulnerability, Morgen met his gaze. "I will not marry a son of Carlow."

The king cocked an eyebrow and his lips thinned—a sure sign his rage was building. The king was a fearsome man when he was angered, which was quite often when it came to Morgen. She managed to swallow her fear. "You have always spoken against that royal family." The strength present in her voice pleased her. She gambled with the king's mood and continued with her pursuit to understand why he would send her to the Kingdom of Carlow. Even though he did not want her as a daughter, he would not want to provide anything to the hated neighboring kingdom. Morgen held his gaze and demanded answer without apology. "Why do you want me to wed into that royal family?"

"The Red Caps knock at our door." He pointed toward the southwest corner of the room. "Would you rather live with them when they breach our border?"

She shuddered at the thought of being under control of the vicious creatures. Their kingdom lay in the direction the king gestured, south of the shared boundary with Carlow. They had infiltrated through the strong border surrounding Carlow just months ago, waging a harsh battle that left many dead. It was shocking that the Red Caps, who thrived on pain and the drawing of blood, had allied themselves with the normally peace-loving gnomes. Yet, that alliance had allowed the Red Caps to access the technical skills of the gnomes and manage the feat. News of the battle had sent shockwaves through the royal household of Meath. Morgen's childhood fears of the Red Caps resurfaced, practically paralyzing her with the thought of facing the horrifying green-skinned creatures, their caps soaked in and dripping with bright red blood.

The king saw her reaction and sneered. "You have been nothing but a burden your entire meager life. Your only asset, at least in this case, is that you are female. The spawn of Carlow requires a wife and the king, fool that he is, has agreed to take you on. You are to keep your kingdom safe by securing an alliance with Carlow."

"And if I refuse?" She crossed her arms over her chest.

King Tobin leaned even further toward her with his feet planted firmly on the marble floor. His large hands gripped the heavily carved arm rests so tightly his fingers turned white. His eyes sparked with anger and his expression distorted his features into a gruesome mask. "You have no grounds to refuse. I am your king and you will do my bidding. For once, Fruhlingsmorgen, you will do something to benefit your kingdom."

Morgen gritted her teeth at his use of her full name. She hated when he used it, because it meant she had pushed him too far. Throughout her nineteen years, the sound of her full name usually preceded some form of physical discipline. Holding her breath, she waited for him to leap from his perch and punish her with his meaty fist. Her left cheek still bore the colors from her last encounter with his anger. She couldn't seem to help herself. She wanted to stand up to this man who worked relentlessly to tamp down her spirit when he should be protecting her instead. At least, that is what a good father did. So she heard.

"You will leave for the border in two days' time."

She opened her mouth to argue.

"Cease your questions. I tire of your voice."

She refused to back away when he stood and took two steps

toward her, although her heart beat so hard she was sure it could be seen through her boned bodice and corset. The king stopped and stared at her with his hands curled into fists. Morgen drew in a stabilizing breath and refused to look away from his intense stare. The anger in his eyes increased. "I am glad to be rid of you. Prepare to depart in the morning."

"You said I would leave in two days."

"I changed my mind." The even tone of his voice was more terrifying than his roar. She didn't flinch as the king stalked past her and out of view trailed by his hangers-on and sycophants. With a sigh, she turned and caught the eye of Beatrice, the woman who was privy to all her secrets and dreams. As Morgen's governess, Beatrice was instrumental in teaching her manners and deportment, as well as her scholastic education. It was due to her diligent instruction that the princess was proficient at numbers and several languages, including gnomenclature and the guttural language of the Red Caps. She hoped never to use that particular expertise, yet with their continual attacks against the nearby fairy kingdoms, they were a prominent aspect of her life. She had also taught Morgen that a true family supported and loved each other. The princess imagined what it would have been like to grow up in a world where her father loved her, her mother lived, and her brother saw her as a playmate rather than a competitor. It would have been the complete opposite of the life she had endured in the gilded palace of Meath.

Morgen struggled to ensure her face was composed in an

expressionless mask, as her eyes shined with unshed tears. Beatrice watched her with compressed lips until the king's voice could no longer be heard thundering through the spacious corridors of the palace. Once it faded, Morgen walked to Beatrice's side and together they walked through the corridors to the princess' small suite of rooms. They stayed silent, knowing there were ears around every corner and amongst the small groups of courtiers that dotted their route. Any one of them would be happy to report their words to the king.

Once away from the prying eyes of court with the door to her sitting room carefully closed and locked, Morgen went straight to her window seat and hugged a tasseled pillow to her chest. Here, in the safety of her rooms, she could allow her emotions to emerge and her tears to fall. Beatrice came to her side and knelt before her on the plush floral rug as her tears flowed in a seemingly unending torrent. As exhaustion settled over her, Morgen took comfort from the weight of her friend's hand on her knee.

"This will be an adventure. Can you not see how exciting this will be?"

Morgen blinked to clear her vision and swiped at her cheeks as she stared into her companion's beautiful cornflower blue eyes. Emotions welled up within her at the thought of life without Beatrice's steady influence. "Will you go to Carlow with me?"

Beatrice's expression fell slightly as she shook her head. "I cannot."

"I need you."

"You need only yourself."

Morgen slipped from the window seat to the floor beside Beatrice and gripped her friend's hands. "I cannot be in such an unfamiliar place without you. I need a friendly face at my side."

Beatrice smiled and extricated her hands from Morgen's grip. "I hear Prince Stephen is a handsome lad. You can gaze upon his countenance."

Tears continued to slip down Morgen's cheeks. "Please do not tease me. I am so frightened."

"I am sorry." She pulled her into an embrace. "It is impossible for me to accompany you."

"Why?"

"I have been discharged."

Morgen let out a squeak and drew back to look at Beatrice. "What? Why? I need a companion, a chaperone."

She shook her head. "You are a grown woman now. There is no need for me."

Morgen curled forward and clenched her hands as despair coursed through her. Everything she cared about was being stripped from her. She would soon be in a strange kingdom, with no friends around to soften the transition. "How am I to do this? I need you." She looked up at Beatrice. "I shall send for you once I am established in Carlow."

Beatrice's eyes shimmered with unshed tears. "I must stay in Meath. My parents need my help. The farm is becoming too much for them to handle."

A sob clogged Morgen's throat at the finality of her words. She knew family was the most important thing to Beatrice and she had been without hers for too long while she served as Morgen's governess. It made sense she would return home to be with her parents. With a nod, Morgen gathered her emotions tightly around her. "Yes, you must go to them. No doubt they will welcome your presence." She looked out the window. "I will write to you about my experiences in Carlow, if that is allowed."

"Of course, it will be allowed, Morgen. Do not fall to your dramatics. It is a terrible habit of yours."

She let out a soft laugh. Beatrice always seemed to know when she needed to be reined in. "See? I continue to have need for you." She shook her head as Beatrice began to speak. "No, I understand that you have responsibilities elsewhere. I must learn to rely on myself without my Beatrice." Morgen continued to grip her governess' hands, knowing she could no longer depend on her governess' steadying influence. "I must learn to stand on my own, without you." She looked about her rooms. "And I must pack."

"Would you like my help?"

She grinned and released Beatrice's hands. "Will that undermine my quest for independence?"

Her soft laughter settled about her like a familiar cloak. "Not at all. I will gather my own belongings first and then return here."

"Are you leaving so soon?"

"I depart the palace alongside you in the morning."

Morgen's mood deflated. "You are tarred with the same brush

as myself."

She shrugged. "With you gone, there is no reason for me to stay."

The princess nodded, but couldn't forgive the callous dismissal of her most-beloved friend. Beatrice deserved so much more honor than this wave of the hand and demand to leave the palace. "I hope you know how much you mean to me."

"I do."

"I may never see you after I leave here."

She nodded. Morgen willed her tears not to fall and attempted to distract herself from this bleak line of thought. She cleared her throat and forced a smile to her lips. "How will you travel to the farmlands?"

"I shall fly."

"With your valises?"

Beatrice smiled. "I expect I will need only one. Once my gowns are miniaturized there is not much more to fill the bag."

"But you have lived here for so long."

"Yes, sixteen years. I came when you were three years old."

"I remember that day."

"You were so upset."

Morgen shrugged.

"It was a slow process for us to become friends."

"It was. You scared me."

"You scared *me*. You were such a headstrong little thing."

Morgen grimaced. "I still am."

Beatrice reached out and touched a light finger to the green and yellow bruise on Morgen's cheek. "Yes." She peered into her eyes with a gentle smile. "There is an upside to this engagement."

"Is there?"

She nodded. "It removes you from your father's attentions. That is a good thing."

Morgen shrugged. "Perhaps."

"Not perhaps. Absolutely." Beatrice put her arm around Morgen's waist and pulled her close. "You have always yearned to leave the borders of Meath, to explore what lies in the kingdoms beyond."

Morgen turned her face to the tall windows that looked out upon the side gardens of the palace. As she gazed at the green herbs and vegetables that had been coaxed from the ground she thought about her childhood dreams to travel. "I imagined it being on my own terms." She turned to look at Beatrice. "With you by my side."

She smiled. "You did not dream of your groom awaiting your arrival?"

"I never imagined being married."

"We have discussed this particular subject many times. As a royal princess, you are expected to marry into a royal family in order to serve your kingdom."

"I know." She rose to her feet and stepped away from Beatrice's reassuring touch as the evening light faded into darkness. "I did not expect it so soon. I had so much more to see, to accomplish, before I became subject to my husband's rule."

Beatrice came to stand beside her, but did not put an arm about her. "There are times when our destiny does not align with our personal plans."

She threw her arms around her beloved governess and buried her face in her shoulder. "I need you."

Beatrice extricated herself from Morgen's embrace. "You have all the knowledge you require." She cupped her cheek with her hand and smiled. "You are a fine person. Thoughtful and true." As Morgen smiled, she removed her hand and turned away. "It becomes late. I need to go to my bed chamber to gather my belongings. Choose what you want to bring with you." Morgen watched her cross the floor, then turn at the door and look at her. "Remember, you will not be allowed to keep any items from Meath, aside from a small wardrobe that will be quickly replaced upon your arrival. All must be left behind."

Morgen caught her lower lip between her teeth as the door closed behind her governess. She glanced around her sitting room as blood pounded in her ears. Her most precious treasures were housed in this room. The shelves were laden with the bits and bobs she had gathered along her nineteen years. How was she to abandon them? Morgen's knees threatened to buckle as she looked at the spines of her books, remembering the hours of escape she found within their pages. The stories and the characters that filled her head with adventures and mysteries had helped make life within the palace bearable. She wanted to bring them with her to ease the transition from Meath to Carlow.

Now, with marriage to a royal son in her future, she would not be allowed to have these friends at her side. Tears slid silently down her cheeks as she stroked her fingertips across the bindings of her books and the cool ceramic of her collection of painted animals, stars, and seashells. She loathed to leave it all behind, but knew it was required. She was expected to sever all ties to her former home and kingdom to display full commitment to her bridegroom's monarchy.

With a sigh, she conjured a drawstring bag in her signature color of cerise pink. Her namesake rose was the same color and all her gowns, cloaks, and footwear were in the same brilliant pink. Her rose also boasted a hint of yellow with maroon stamens, and these hues accented her clothing and items as well. She waved her hand over her books to miniaturize them and sent them into the bag. Her ceramic treasures followed. She drew the maroon cording and gathered the top closed. She selected three gowns carefully, changing her mind and reforming her gowns multiple times as she tried to decide which to bring with her to Carlow. Finally, she made her final decision and rounded out her wardrobe with shoes, petticoats, and ribbons.

Determined not to change her mind again, she sent the valise filled with her clothing floating across the room to settle by her door. She left the drawstring bag on the settee, next to her favorite book as a knock sounded through the sitting room. Beatrice smiled when she opened the door.

"Come in." Morgen stepped to the side.

"Do you need any help?"

"No."

Beatrice stood in the middle of the room and turned in a slow circle. "This is difficult."

"Yes." Morgen closed the door with a firm click and crossed the room to pick up the drawstring bag. "This is for you. To fill out the library of your family home."

She accepted the bag and pulled it open. "Oh, Your Highness, this is too much."

Morgen held up her hands to ward off the bag her governess tried to return and shook her head. "They must go where they will be appreciated. You know they will not find a happy home here at the palace."

Beatrice inclined her head in agreement and peered into the depths of the bag again. "Your ceramics." She pulled out a tiny rabbit figurine. It lay small and white in her palm as she searched Morgen's expression. With a curt nod she lowered it back into the bag. "I will care for these and remember our precious time together."

Morgen picked up the book she had not miniaturized and held it out to her. "You must take this as well."

Beatrice drew the drawstrings shut with a snap. "No. That is your favorite."

"I will not be allowed to keep it."

"You need it for your journey."

Morgen looked down at the gilt lettering. "Then what? I cannot cross the border with it. It will be tossed into the pig sty." She looked back at her face. "Please. It deserves the best of homes. That is with you."

Beatrice frowned and extended her hand to accept the book. "I will think of you with each word I read."

Morgen blinked away the tears in her eyes as she watched the book miniaturize and disappear into the depths of the bag. She was truly without any of her personal treasures.

Beatrice placed a hand gently on her arm. "Come, let us sit and discuss tomorrow."

She followed her to the settee, grateful for the brief opportunity to gather her emotions. She didn't want to think about tomorrow and her departure from Meath. She sat close to Beatrice. "I am to marry a son of Carlow. How is this possible?"

Beatrice held Morgen's hand and clasped it between her palms. Morgen was grateful for her support, knowing she could not indulge in her desire to crawl into bed and hide under the covers. "I wish you could go with me." She shook her head as Beatrice opened her mouth to speak. "I know, you cannot. That does not stop me from wishing it could be different."

"This is something you must navigate on your own." She squeezed her hand. "You will do well."

"I am not so sure." She allowed herself to slouch against the back of the settee as misery washed over her. "Do you think they will permit my rose to be planted amongst those of the Carlowian royal family?"

"We have discussed your propensity toward the dramatic."

Morgen looked down at her hands. "I am not optimistic about my future."

"You should be. This is going to be an exciting adventure."

She shrugged.

"You cannot imagine having an interesting life there?"

She shook her head.

"Forget what you have learned from your father, and even your brother. Remember what I have taught you about Carlow."

Morgen tried, but could remember nothing but the scornful descriptions of her father. He must be right. She trusted Beatrice more than any other fairy, yet she couldn't imagine her father negotiating an alliance that would be to her benefit. Unless—

"Is the threat from the Red Caps so severe he would choose to improve my situation by forming an alliance with Carlow?"

Beatrice stopped talking and stared at her.

"My apologies for interrupting, but I must know." She leaned toward her. "Would he?"

"I cannot speak for the king."

"Yes, but—"

Beatrice held a finger to Morgen's lips, urging her to remain silent. "However, I can speculate."

Morgen held her breath as she paused and folded her hands in her lap.

"The king would do nothing in benefit of you."

"Which means the Red Cap threat is strong enough that he is

willing to send me to Carlow." She grasped Beatrice's hands. "They may be breaching our border this very minute." She glanced at the darkened sky and then back to her governess. "Keep yourself safe. Promise me."

"I will." She leaned forward and kissed Morgen's cheek. "Now, let us talk of happier things." Morgen allowed Beatrice to steer the conversation to their many adventures together. By the time the first fingers of dawn streaked across the sky, Morgen was laughing at Beatrice's animated recounting of their happier memories.

As the laughter faded, Beatrice stood and shook out her skirts. "You need to have a few hours' rest before your departure."

"I do not need to sleep. Please stay."

She shook her head. "You have a busy day ahead of you. Sleep is a must for you, as it is for me. I have a far fly this morning."

Morgen frowned. Her words were filled with wisdom, yet she did not want to miss a single moment with Beatrice. With regret, she acquiesced and watched her friend leave the sitting room.

"I shall return as you prepare for your departure." She picked up the drawstring bag filled with the books and ceramics and hugged it to her chest. "Thank you for this." Her smile warmed Morgen's heart as she watched Beatrice leave the room.

Morgen's lady's maid entered the room to help her ready for the day. Her eyes widened in surprise as she took in the princess' disheveled appearance but quickly regained her composure. Morgen filled the silence between them. "I need to ready for bed." The maid nodded and helped her out of her gown. As Morgen slipped between the sheets, she thought how this would be the last time these blankets would be lifted for her, the last time she would lay on this mattress and look up at the floral canopy that draped above her. After the maid left her room, Morgen closed her eyes and allowed her tears to fall, allowing her pillow to capture her tears for the final time.

A few hours later, Morgen's maid awakened her with a tray filled with tea, scones, and jam. Morgen was exhausted as she carried her plate and teacup to the bathroom and set them within arm's reach on an ornately painted table as she took her bath. Once the water cooled and her fingertips were wrinkled from the water, Morgen rang for her lady's maid. The silent servant held out a drying sheet and she stepped out of the water and into the folds of the chilly fabric. Morgen imagined the maid was looking forward to her departure, but she wondered about the girl's future position in the palace. When she left, the maid would be free of serving the unwanted royal princess, but would also lose the only role that kept her within the palace walls.

Morgen rubbed her skin dry and then allowed the maid to assist her with her corset and petticoats before she donned her finest gown and slippers. After the maid closed the seam of her gown with the tip of her wand, Morgen sat at her dressing table and watched as her hair was curled and twirled into an elaborate braided creation. The maid was just completing curling the long tendrils that would lay against the skin of her exposed neck and shoulders when Beatrice arrived. With a quick curtsey, the maid left the room and Morgen slid off the stool and twirled before her governess.

"Do I look well enough?"

"You look beautiful. Will you wear your formal cloak?"

"Yes." She indicated the cloak draped over the back of an upholstered wingchair. "I need to look my best for my flight to the border. The Carlowian knights will be waiting to escort me through the border."

"My dear, you will not fly to the border."

"How will I get there?"

"By carriage, as befitting a princess."

Morgen nodded even as her heart sank at the idea of the long ride.

To Morgen's surprise, the king's best carriage awaited her as she and Beatrice stepped out the front doors of the palace and emerged onto the drive. She knew this was not for her own comfort, but for his image. Her father wanted the kingdoms of Meath and Carlow to think he was reluctant to marry off his only daughter. Yet, he did not make an appearance to bid her farewell. Nor did her brother. Morgen was relieved, even as disappointment flitted through her. The two were likely seated in the family suite, awaiting news her departure. She imagined the king was relieved to be rid of her, and her brother was glad to rid himself of a presumed rival for their father's attention. Although, what he had to be concerned about, she had no idea. The king had never shown her anything but dismissal and contempt.

As she and Beatrice emerged from under the portico, a footman opened the carriage door and stood motionless, his gaze aimed relentlessly down the drive to the gates. She ignored his silent message to leave without delay and turned to pull Beatrice into an embrace.

"Promise you will write to me."

Beatrice nodded. "Ping if you need anything."

Morgen nodded, too overwhelmed by her emotions to speak. She welcomed the request to send a mental message to her friend, knowing it would result in her image being flashed in Beatrice's mind and her words sounding in her head. They had not used the ability often, but she had relied on the private conversations during the tortuous meetings with her family.

"Keep yourself open to adventure." Beatrice pulled her into a tighter embrace. "And make sure you let me know how you are. Do you hear me?"

She nodded against her shoulder. "I shall ping you before I cross the border. After that--"

"I know. You will be out of reach."

"I will be limited to letters once I am in Carlow." Emotion overwhelmed her. A sob tore from her as she hugged Beatrice again. She gripped her shoulders with shaking hands. "I will write you often."

"We are sisters, you and I."

Morgen tried to compose herself, but could not stop another sob from filling the air. She gave up any attempt at a serene countenance as Beatrice pulled her into another embrace and kissed her cheek.

"No matter the distance between us, we will remain sisters. I love you."

Morgen refused to release her governess from her embrace and let out a small cry. "Please say you will visit me. Please."

Beatrice moved to extricate herself from the embrace and Morgen loosened her grip. "I will visit you as soon as I can." She shifted her valise from one hand to the other. "Now, I must depart. My parents await me at the farm and your future is across the border."

Morgen nodded and stepped away. Her cheeks were wet with tears and her chin trembled as she climbed inside the carriage. Ignoring the drape of her skirts, she lowered the window and leaned out to watch Beatrice extend her wings and take to the air. She would be home within the hour. Morgen watched her friend grow smaller as she flew over the city. The carriage lurched forward and moved down the drive toward the ornate front gates of the palace. The painted and gilded wheels crunched over the packed gravel and the horses nickered in the still air. Morgen leaned out the window even further to keep Beatrice in sight.

"Good bye," she pinged.

Beatrice returned the farewell as the mist swallowed her form and Morgen rode into the streets of the Kingdom of Meath's capitol city. None of her father's subjects lined the street to bid farewell to their princess. Saddened, but also thankful she did not need to hide her emotions, Morgen slid the window shut and leaned back against the tufted velvet cushions. As she swayed with the movement of the carriage, her tears began to fall.

Long after the city had disappeared behind her, Morgen rested her head against a small pillow and gave in to the soothing rocking of the carriage. She dreamed of afternoons spent laying amongst sun-warmed flowers in a wide meadow. Birds sang sweet songs from their perches in the trees bordering the meadow and she could hear the soothing sound of running water. A bee buzzed close to her ear and continued on its way. A flower tickled her cheek. She smiled as absolute serenity surrounded her.

The sun was beginning to approach the western horizon when she awakened. Disoriented, she pulled open a fringed shade and looked out the window. Endless trees surrounded her in every direction. She wasn't familiar with this area of the kingdom, but assumed she was close to the meeting spot. Morgen opened the brown leather carriage box, but the clock had not been wound. Still, she needed to prepare to meet the Carlowian knights and cross the border. She lifted a small mirror from its nest in the box and peered into it. Her hair was difficult to see in the diminutive reflection, but she saw a few stray strands to pat into place. After pinching her cheeks and smoothing her skirts, Morgen returned the mirror to the box and pulled open the remaining window shades.

As she smoothed the last crease from her skirts, the carriage came to a lurching halt. Her heart pounded in her chest as the door opened and a handsome knight dressed in a charcoal gray overcoat poked his head inside and smiled stiffly at her. The starched collar of a snowy white shirt caught the fading evening light. "Princess Fruhlingsmorgen, we are happy to meet you. I am Sir Thomas of Carlow."

She considered him for a moment. He was young and appeared friendly, but his words were terse. These barbarians had the appearance of gentlemen, but she knew they were under orders to be well-mannered. Likely, they would have preferred to slit her throat than assist her through the border. "Please call me Princess Morgen."

He bowed and unfolded the steps of the carriage. Morgen cast her gaze to the Knights of Meath, but they did not appear concerned, either for her safety or her future. She was on her own even as the trappings of her king surrounded her.

"Beatrice!" she pinged.

Her governess' image flashed behind Morgen's eyes. "All is well." Her tone was soothing. Beatrice obviously heard the panic in her voice. "You are a princess of Meath."

Ignoring the knight's proffered hand, Morgen alighted from the carriage independently. She needed them to know she was a self-confident and assured woman and not cowed by her situation. It would not do to let these Carlowian knights see how nervous she was in their company.

"Please come with me." A Meathian knight gestured to the

border, which shimmered before her.

She pinged her goodbye to Beatrice, regretting the loss of this comforting form of communication. Attempting to appear as regal and self-confident as possible, Morgen placed her hand on the Meathian knight's arm and walked with him through her kingdom's border and into the isolated area between Meath and Carlow. It was an odd sensation, to be surrounded and filled with the energy field that protected her kingdom. Now, she was nowhere. This small area, only a few feet across, belonged to no kingdom and was not protected. This transfer was the reason for the presence of the knights. She stepped across the dirt ground and stood before the border into Carlow. She would not attempt the crossing without the approved Carlowian as her escort. The protective characteristics of the border would likely cause an excruciating death for anyone who attempted the crossing without the required permissions.

"If you please." A Carlowian knight, different than the man who opened the carriage door, extended his arm. She rested her hand on the fine wool sleeve of his greatcoat and held her breath as they crossed into Carlow. A faint glow of energy filled her as the border surrounded and then fell behind her.

She was in Carlow.

Chapter Two

A handsome black and red carriage sat squarely on the packed dirt road before Morgen. The top two-thirds of the main body and doors were black, outlined with gold. The bottom third was a regal red, the panels edged with a fine line of gold. Sparkling gold finials marched along the length and width of the roofline and the wheel spokes were black and edged in gold. She could see the seal of the royal family of Carlow, the Mulryans, emblazoned on the door. Six matching grays stomped the ground as cloudy air shrouded their muzzles with each exhale. Morgen burrowed deeper into her cloak as cold air snaked through her. She guessed it was at least twenty degrees colder here in Carlow than just across the border in Meath.

"Welcome to Carlow, Your Royal Highness." The knight who escorted her through the border turned away and walked ahead of her to the carriage. Offended by the slight, Morgen remained in place as he opened the door and stepped to the side.

"If you please." He gestured from her to the steps that had been unfolded and allowed for easy access to the interior of the ornate vehicle.

Morgen paused to express her displeasure and then slowly made her way to the carriage. She ignored his proffered hand and grasped the handle engraved with climbing roses. Once inside, she sat in the middle of the oversized cushioned armchair that lined the rear of the compartment and fluffed her skirts. She refused to lean against the padded back rest. Morgen was determined to uphold the standards of manners that were instilled since birth. She was, after all, a princess of Meath.

Unable to curb her curiosity, she peeked through the rear window and saw her small valise being carried through the border. She knew it had been inspected by the knights in search of contraband. Morgen blushed at the thought of these knights pawing through her intimates. She had considered hiding a book or a crystal within the bag's depths, but decided against it. She was glad of her foresight. It would have been found and taken. A clunk behind her head told her the valise had been stowed up top with the rear footman.

With a sigh, she shifted her weight on the bench and waited to begin her journey to the capital city of Revlin, the palace, and her intended. The Carlowian knights mounted their own beautiful gray stallions and drew alongside the carriage as it started forward with a jolt. Morgen kept her gaze straight ahead and stared at a button that tufted the cushions on the opposite padded armchair. Through her peripheral vision, she tried to catch a knight glancing in her direction, but not one paid any attention to her. They kept their heads turned toward the dense forest on either side of the carriageway or straight ahead. Apparently, they were as uninterested in her as she was curious about them. She allowed another sigh to pass through her lips as she directed her attention back to the button.

Her back ached and her eyes drooped with fatigue when they finally passed through the gates that marked the main thoroughfare into the capitol city of Revlin. The full moon was bright and illuminated the ornate black and gold ironworks of the gate. Small cottages that had dotted the woods outside the gates gave way to larger homes as the carriageway widened. Morgen longed to leave the conveyance and walk on solid, unshifting ground, or, even better, unfurl her wings and take flight. She longed for the feel of the wind sliding over her face and arms, and the freedom to swoop amongst the treetops.

As she imagined herself aloft, a bright light illuminated the interior of the carriage. Morgen turned away and pulled her wand from the pocket of air next to her. As she prepared to defend herself, she saw fairies lining both sides of the road, waving to her. Some stood at the roadside and some hovered behind them. Others lined the awnings, windows, and rooftops of the surrounding buildings. Balls of light illuminated the interior of the carriage, dragged from the brilliant moon and thrown by the fairies lining the road. They were casting light to see her. Morgen smiled and waved. Each time her hand rose in their direction, the fairies cheered. She was astonished at the welcome. Never had she experienced such a warm reception as this.

As the carriage turned a sharp corner, the palace caught her attention. Ablaze in lights, the impressive building dominated the end of the avenue. Golden stone glowed and cast interesting shadows across the face of the looming palace. An ornate fence surrounded the grounds; purely ornamental since any fairy who wished to enter the royal residence had only to fly over its height. Of course, knights protected the palace and the monarch with veracity. Morgen bit her lower lip. That was how things were done in Meath. She wondered if it was the same here in Carlow.

Absently, she continued to wave at the crowds, which had thickened considerably as she approached the palace. She touched her braided hair and smoothed her palm over any visible creases in her skirts. She had little knowledge of the protocols that ruled Carlow, let alone how they performed their daily tasks and chores. Her education was broad and personal, thanks to Beatrice's teachings, but did not prepare her for life outside the borders of Meath.

Finally, and too soon, the carriage entered the ornate black and gold gates of the palace. Morgen tried not to gawk, but it was difficult. The palace was impressive and spoke of the kingdom's wealth and status. As they drove around to the inner courtyard, she saw a carpet that rolled out from a deeply carved black door sheltered by a portico. The cherry pink runner extended into the drive and the carriage halted with the door perfectly aligned. Morgen was touched the carpet was in her signature color, even down to the yellow edging.

The carriage door opened and the steps were lowered. A masculine hand marred by small age spots on its back extended into the interior. The braiding on the cuff signified this was not one of the knights that had accompanied her on the journey, but someone higher in the palace hierarchy.

"Princess Fruhlingsmorgen, welcome to Carlow."

She placed her hand into that of the older gentlefairy and stepped out onto the carpet.

"I am the Lord Chamberlain."

Morgen nodded to him and rested her hand on his arm as he accompanied her to the palace door. Maroon curls swirled through the pink carpet with each footfall and disappeared, leaving a smooth surface behind her.

"We expected your arrival tomorrow, but we were able to make adjustments. The royal family awaits you in the throne room."

"Thank you." She worked to keep her hand still and light on his arm, instead of gripping it in a fit of nerves. Anxiety swirled through her and the Lord Chamberlain slowed his pace as they walked through a highly-arched corridor washed in a gentle blue.

Candles flickered in sconces between crystalline windows, each bordered with snowy white drapes. Everything was accented in gold. It was breathtaking, even with the darkened night sky outside.

"Here is the throne room."

Morgen stayed in the corridor as the Lord Chamberlain rapped twice with his silver-capped black walking stick and then entered the room. The two following raps of the stick on the hardwood parquet floor echoed through the empty corridor as Morgen drew in a stabilizing breath and closed her eyes as she recalled Beatrice's soothing words.

"Your Majesties. Your Royal Highness. The Princess Fruhlingsmorgen of the Kingdom of Meath."

A rustle of fabric reached her ears as she waited the customary count of ten before entering the room. Ensuring she wore a pleasant expression, Morgen walked into the lovely room of state. Expecting only the royal family, she was surprised, and slightly horrified, to see the spacious room filled to capacity with brightly-dressed nobility. Hundreds of pairs of eyes scrutinized and assessed her as she walked toward the Lord Chamberlain. She worked to maintain a neutral expression as she returned to the Lord Chamberlain's side and rested her hand on his arm. Her hand shook and she was sure her face was pale as they approached the raised dais upon which two thrones were solidly placed.

"We had expected you tomorrow."

She looked toward the booming voice and the handsome couple

seated upon the ornate thrones. Four younger fairies, three boys and a girl, stood next to Their Majesties the King and Queen. She was sure one of them was her intended, yet she did not know which one.

She curtseyed deeply before the thrones. "I apologize, Your Majesties, for my untimely arrival. The King of Meath commanded that I arrive today."

As the king surveyed her and conversed with the queen, Morgen turned her attention to the male fairy standing directly to the right of the king. He was most likely the heir to the throne. She estimated him to be about six feet tall with the broad shoulders of a knight. His frock coat and dark trousers were finely cut and fit him well. She could see his dark hair was a deep chestnut brown, but could not make out the color of his eyes, apart from their appearing light. He was a handsome man. She hoped he found her appearance pleasing.

"Your Royal Highness." Her voice was pleasant and she made sure she smiled with her greeting.

He bowed but declined to speak. When he turned to converse with the fairies beside him, likely to be his brothers, Morgen moved her attention to the remainder of people on the dais. Aside from the king and queen and the three sons, Morgen was happy to see the younger girl, likely the royal princess, who appeared to be close to her own age. She was the image of her mother with long blonde locks and light eyes. Her smile was genuine and illuminated her face. She was beautiful. Morgen hoped she would become a friend.

The far end of the dais was filled with two male fairies the approximate age of the king, and their families. Judging from their proximity to the monarch and their placement on the royal dais, they were likely the king's brothers and sisters, accompanied by their children, the lesser princesses. Three lovely girls in pale pink gowns appeared to be the approximate age of the youngest royal son. Two of them held fans before their faces and whispered to each other as they watched her. Judging from their behavior, she did not meet their standards. With work, her smile did not falter.

"We are honored to have you in our kingdom."

At the sound of the king's commanding voice, she turned back to him and bobbed a curtsey. "Your welcoming presence is my honor."

"May we introduce Her Majesty Queen Claire?"

She turned her eyes to the radiant woman dressed in an elegant gown of snowy white. Diamonds twinkled at her throat and were woven through her hair. She was truly beautiful.

"It is my honor to be in your presence."

The queen smiled and became even more radiant.

"Here is our son, His Royal Highness Prince Stephen."

Her intended! He was indeed the son who stood closest to the king. Morgen curtseyed to him, unable to look away when the other two princes were introduced. She barely registered the names Edward and Rupert. However, while she was smitten with his dashing figure, he did not appear to return the feeling. He bowed low with a serious expression that did not alter as he scrutinized her. Morgen's smile slipped slightly as she turned her attention back to the king and queen. She did not want to interrupt their quiet conversation, but could not leave the room without their permission.

"It was a pleasure to meet with you." She curtseyed to the king and queen and the royal princes and princesses.

The royal couple turned their attention back to her. "We are pleased to have you here." The queen nodded her agreement. "We look forward to learning more about you."

Morgen curtseyed.

"Excuse me, Princess Fruhlingsmorgen?"

"My Lord Chamberlain."

"If you will come with me, I will show you to your rooms."

Maintaining her composure in the face of the continuing scrutiny from the royal princes and princess, the lesser royals, and the surrounding peers of the realm, Morgen walked from the throne room on the arm of the Lord Chamberlain. He led her through a maze of corridors until she was completely turned around. All the doors looked alike, the same paint was on all the walls and the same red and gold carpeting muffled her footfalls as she walked through the palace. Thoroughly lost, Morgen blindly walked with the Lord Chamberlain through the turns and twists and up two grand staircases. She was pleased with the gracious manners of the Lord Chamberlain, who was the senior fairy in the Royal Household. He would be the primary organizer of her wedding day.

"My Lor—"

"Here is your door. Oh, my apologies, Princess." He appeared mortified to have spoken over her.

Morgen smiled. "It was not important."

"Everything you have to say is extremely important."

He looked sincere, but Morgen wasn't sure if he was being facetious or speaking his true feelings. This was Carlow, after all. She need to remain on alert for smooth talkers and charlatans. Yet, due to his high rank and status as a royal advisor, she needed to maintain a positive relationship with this particular member of the royal household. "Thank you for taking the time during these late hours to show me to my rooms. I appreciate your thoughtfulness."

He bowed low and waited in the corridor until she entered the room and closed the door behind her. She put her ear to the polished panel door and listened for his retreating footfalls. There was silence for a moment, and then she could discern the sound of his retreat. She wondered about the pause, questioning if he stood outside her door in concern for her safety or to ensure she was in place for the night.

Morgen closed her eyes and leaned her forehead against the door. No matter the kindness extended to her, she must remember the vicious atrocities and acts of barbarism that occurred in this forsaken kingdom. As voices sounded from the corridor outside her door, she reached down and twisted the lock into place before wandering through the room before her. It was a lovely sitting room with plush appointments and tall windows. She ran her fingers along the light-colored fabric covered with roses that upholstered a cushioned wing chair. A matching settee was positioned at a right angle to the chair and its mate, with small tables of light maple between them. A rectangular tea table occupied the open space before them, set upon a thick rug of the same light color and bordered by roses. A fireplace dominated the wall that the comfortable arrangement faced. It was dark and cold, without a fire to warm the rooms. She frowned at the oversight and stepped to the windows. In the moonlight, she could see manicured gardens that sloped from a large stone terrace below her. A fountain anchored the base of the gentle slope and beyond she could see a large rectangular lake.

"Beautiful." Her breath clouded the panes and she drew her finger through the condensation. She would need warmer clothing sooner than she expected. Carlow was very different from Meath.

She turned away from the window and went through another door. It led to a plush bedroom with a canopied bed. A thick comforter and large pillows dominated the expansive mattress, with carved roses climbing the wooden posts that supported the canopy. More of the same fabric that covered the wing chairs was gathered in the interior of the canopy and draped to the floor, held to the wall by plush golden tassels. Highly-polished night tables in the same light wood as the side tables in the sitting room flanked the bed. A beautifully carved armoire and dresser occupied the opposite walls. Next to the armoire was a dressing table with a flounced chair. Two small cushioned wing chairs were settled next to a small table before the window, providing a lovely spot to have her morning or evening tea while admiring the gardens and lake.

Morgen went through an adjoining door. It led to a smaller room that was dominated by a clawfoot bathtub in the middle of the floor. The walls were covered in a subtly striped wallpaper and the entire room was light and airy. It was beautiful. She longed for a bath now, but the servants were likely abed. She glanced through the door to the bedroom and saw a clock tucked into a corner. It was early morning. She would wait until a more reasonable hour to request hot water. Instead, she would use her time to care for her meager wardrobe herself, as no lady's maid had yet made an appearance.

Her valise had been brought to the room, likely while she was meeting the extended royal family. It was set on a luxurious chaise lounge at the foot of the bed. The light fabric that covered the decadent piece of furniture was a different rose pattern, the colors here pale pinks and yellows. Green leaves and vines popped as they wound through the nosegays of roses. The back arm of the chaise lounge was carved into a graceful swan's neck. Morgan stroked the smoothly polished wood, surprised with the opulence of the suite. Part of her had expected the dungeon or something at least a bit more sparse. She was, after all, a daughter of Meath. This warm welcome by the palace and the subject of the kingdom was unexpected.

A thought niggled at the back of her mind. She wondered if the stories she had heard about the barbarism of Carlow were filled with truth. Morgen shook her head at the thought. The knowledge was so pervasive, so known throughout Meath, it was impossible to think that they were all lies. They couldn't be so completely woven into the foundation of Meathian society without having even the smallest kernel of truth.

"I must be too tired if my mind goes down these paths."

Alone in her rooms, Morgen directed all her energies to caring for her thin wardrobe. With her wand in hand, she re-formed her gowns and directed them to the armoire. Knowing her maid would care for the gowns and smooth the creases from the fabrics, Morgen hung three day dresses from hooks and lay her favorite evening gown on a long shelf. The silks and satins shimmered in the lamplight. She allowed herself a moment to admire their beauty before she turned her attention to the remaining items in her valise. Her shoes and boots were sent to the lower shelf and her intimates were tucked into the drawer above. She sent her nightgown, robe, and warm slippers to the chaise lounge.

Stifling a yawn, Morgen attempted to undo the back seam of her travel gown. Under normal circumstances her lady's maid would assist her, but no one was with her tonight. She contorted her body and managed to touch her wand down the length of the seam without too much stress on the delicate fabric. She thought how useful the lower classes made their gowns, with laces up the back and front instead of the seams that required a touch of the wand. They could dress and undress without assistance, whereas she was forced to rely on a lady's maid, or else contort her body and strain her shoulder to the point of pain in order to release herself from the confines of the gown. After she floated her gown, wilted from a day travelling in a carriage, over her head, she left it puddled on the floor. Her petticoats quickly followed and billowed over the gown's cherry pink fabric. Morgen watched the starched fabric collapse and hide the gown's brilliant color from view before adding her corset, underclothes, and stockings to the growing pile.

She took a deep breath, her first since donning her corset that morning. It was difficult to believe she had been back in Meath with her beloved Beatrice this same day. No, yesterday. This was early morning, the beginning of her first full day in Carlow. After a long glance at the bathroom door, wishing for a cleansing bath, she donned her nightgown and sighed. A long soak would do much to ease the tension in her shoulders and back. Instead, she pulled back the covers and climbed into the decadent bed. As the mattress embraced her, exhaustion took hold and Morgen blew out the wall sconces with a puff of air in their direction. In the safety of the bed chamber, with the sheet and duvet pulled up to her chin, the loneliness of her situation overwhelmed her. Turning onto her side, she clenched the soft sheet in her fists and closed her eyes. Her isolation pressed hard upon her and squeezed the first of a flood of tears from her. Knowing she faced a desolate life, Morgen wept into her pillow, wishing she could talk to Beatrice. She didn't want to be engaged to the crowned prince of Carlow. She didn't want to continue to be the unwanted princess, as she had been throughout her life in Meath. She was tired of being the outsider.

Chapter Three

Morgen awakened at her normal early hour, feeling almost as exhausted as she had when she climbed into the bed several hours before. She had forgotten to close the draperies along the windows and around her bed, allowing a bright shaft of light to slant across her eyes and awaken her. As the colors of dawn marked the sky, she pushed back the feather comforter and soft cotton sheets. This was not an optimistic start to the day.

The despondency that had settled over her as she tried to sleep tugged at her, but she did her best to ignore its grip. Today she would find within her the doggedness she had relied upon throughout her life and take the first steps she needed to endure this new situation. Morgen stepped into her slippers, waiting for her body heat to warm them, before moving about her room. She did not know the timing of this new palace but had expected her lady's maid to be present, even at this early hour. Without awaiting her arrival, Morgen quickly washed her face and teeth with the frigid water that filled her pitcher. The drying towel was soft and absorbent as she patted the icy droplets from her skin. If she hadn't been fully awake before, she was now.

She settled on her chaise lounge with her hands folded on her lap for a full thirty minutes before giving up on her maid. She pulled out a day frock from the armoire and spent the next three-quarters of an hour in her chemise, smoothing the wrinkles of the gown's skirts and improving the drape of the fabric. At home, a lady's maid had ensured her gowns were ready for the morning. She had assumed the same would be available here in the wealthier kingdom of Carlow.

"I guess not." She whispered the words even though there was no chance to be heard alone here in her bed chamber.

She pulled on her underclothes and floated the corset around her, but was unable to tighten the laces to draw in her waist. Frustrated, she tried again and again to draw the gap closed but could not contort herself in any way that would allow her to tighten it appropriately. Frustrated, she threw the corset to the floor and glared into the full-length mirror. She drew in a deep breath and pasted a smile to her face to hide her irritation.

"My Lord Chamberlain?" Her ping went unanswered. "Lord Chamberlain?"

"Your Highness?" He sounded breathless and irritated.

Not any less than she. Morgen stood with her hands on her hips. "Please send assistance to my chambers for my morning ministrations."

"My apologies. I will send someone immediately."

Morgen severed the mental link with the man and looked around her bedroom. It was lovely, but showed no sign that a princess of Meath resided within its walls. In a surge of defiance, she pulled out her wand in determination to change that. She altered the fabrics covering the chaise lounge and the dressing table to the more soothing wovens that she loved. She kept one of the small chairs by the window in the light fabric with the roses, liking the airiness of the colors, but darkened the fabric covering the seat of the other. She strode into the sitting room and changed the wood of the tables to the darker hue of her favorite polished walnut. The flimsy chiffon curtains were swapped for a heavier and cozier brocade. With a grin, she did the same to the curtains in the bedroom and darkened the wood of the tables in there as well. The result was a cozy nest that welcomed her into its warm arms.

Back in the sitting room, she draped cashmere throws over the chairs and settee. Their jewel tones nicely complimented the fabrics she had used to cover the furniture and hang at the windows. Satisfied, she plopped down in a wing chair and wrapped a soft and warm crimson throw snugly about her shoulders. As she slipped her wand back into the pocket of air at her side, a light knock sounded at her door.

"Please enter."

A slight fairy slipped inside. With wide eyes, she looked about the room, but remained silent. Morgen smiled, satisfied the changes were noticed.

"Are you here to assist me?"

She nodded and bobbed a curtsey.

"What is your name?"

Her eyes widened even more. "Lily, Your Highness."

"Are you a lady's maid?"

"No, Your Highness."

Morgen tilted her head. It was obvious the nervous little fairy was unused to being recognized by anyone within the royal household.

"What is your position in the palace?"

"I am a housemaid, Your Highness."

Morgen's back stiffened. The Lord Chamberlain had sent her assistance from one of the lowest positions in the household. Only a scullery maid was lower than a housemaid. She looked back at the fairy, who appeared to be her age. "Are you able to assist me in dressing?"

"Yes, Your Highness."

Morgen stood and Lily followed her into the bed chamber. "I

was not able to don my corset alone."

Lily nodded and pulled the laces tight as Morgen held it in place. Once the tails of the laces were tucked away, Morgen raised her arms overhead and Lily floated her petticoats into the air and settled them over her head. The day dress followed. Morgen felt Lily apply the tip of her wand to the back seam until it was closed securely. The skirts fluffed and settled nicely over the petticoats.

"There, Your Highness." Lily attended to the bows at her elbows and down her bodice before she stood before Morgen with her hands clasped and her eyes downcast. "Do you need assistance with your shoes?"

"No, thank you."

The fairy flushed prettily. "P-P-Pardon?"

She smiled. "I said thank you."

Lily curtseyed with a troubled look on her face.

"Is anything the matter?"

She shook her head. "No, Your Highness."

Morgen did not press her further. "I am certain you have other duties to perform. I will not keep you from them." She followed the little maid into the sitting room. Before Lily slipped through the door to the corridor, Morgen called after her, "Do you know who will be my lady's maid?"

"No, Your Royal Highness."

"Thank you."

Lily curtseyed and closed the door quietly behind her. Morgen returned to her bedroom and faced herself in the dressing table mirror. Her hair was still a mess, but she hadn't wanted to cause Lily more anxiety by asking her to dress her hair. Wishing for an experienced and dedicated lady's maid, Morgen sat down before the mirror and smoothed her hair with the silver-backed brush. Once it was woven into a thick braid, she wrapped it into a simple bun at the nape of her neck. Dissatisfied with the effect, but knowing she could do no better, Morgen rose from the chair and promptly tripped over the gown and petticoats she had left on the floor before bed. With a frown, she sent the petticoats to the armoire and shook out the gown. Deep creases marred the fabric. Her slovenly behavior had caused a lot of drudgery for her future maid. She would do better.

Morgen's stomach rumbled unbecomingly as she moved into the sitting room. The hands on the mantle clock told her it was time for breakfast, yet none had arrived. Without assistance, she would not be able to find the dining room. She opened her door and looked both ways down the corridor. No one could be seen. The last thing she wanted to do was wander around the maze of hallways and staircases in search of the dining room. The correct dining room. She imagined a palace this large had several. It would take her until lunch time to find the correct room.

Unwilling to ping the Lord Chamberlain again, she frowned and wrapped the cashmere throw more tightly around her shoulders. It was cold. She glanced at the dark fireplace, wishing for kindling and logs to send warmth into the room. No lady's maid, no breakfast, and no fire. She was an invisible resident of the palace.

Again.

With a sigh, she returned to her bedroom and brought out her gowns and petticoats. With no lady's maid, the state of her meager wardrobe was in her hands. Morgen belled out the skirt of a gown and ran her hands over the creases, smoothing the fabric under the light pressure of her palm. Another gurgling hunger pang filled the air as she longed for breakfast. She attempted to ignore it by continuing with her work.

Once every gown, petticoat, and chemise was smooth and cared for, she straightened the bed clothes. She didn't need to tie back the drapes, since she had forgotten to draw them the night before. With care, she pulled the sheets taut and snugged the duvet into place. After the pillows were fluffed and positioned against the headboard, she stood back with her hands on her hips and admired her work. Her maid back in Meath would be surprised and proud. At the memory of her lilting voice exclaiming, "Janey Mack!", Morgen laughed aloud. With a grin, she returned to the sitting room and considered the paneled door leading to the corridor. She had expected someone to bring a light meal or tea by now. Her grin faded as she considered the possibility that no trays would be delivered to her rooms.

Shards of grief cut through her. She faced the very real possibility of starving to death while living in the luxurious royal household in the wealthiest fairy kingdom.

"Stop falling into your dramatics." She mimicked Beatrice's voice as she said the words aloud. With a plop, she sat on the settee

49

and allowed herself the luxury of leaning back against the cushions. Her stomach rumbled again. She waved her hand limply through the air and conjured a light snack of a scone and a pot of black tea. She didn't want to eat a large meal this close to lunch time. Morgen frowned as she wondered if that meal would be brought to her door, or if a footman would lead her to the dining room. One of the two options must happen. She could not subsist on a diet of conjured food. A fairy could only eat conjured food in an emergency, for a meal or two. It could not sustain anyone over the long run.

Morgen shook her head and enjoyed her repast before sweeping her hand over the tea pot and crumb-covered plate. They disappeared, leaving only a wisp of smoke that quickly dissipated. She walked to the window and watched the cascading waters of the large fountain that stood between the lake and the back terrace below her. Plumes of water shot high into the air and captured the sun. Rainbows shimmered in the mist. She yearned to be out there, in the sunlight with the light breeze and the sound of the falling water.

"Well, why not?"

There was no reason to remain isolated in her rooms. Unwilling to remain a mouse, Morgen donned her warm cloak and stepped out onto the small balcony outside her sitting room windows. The cool mid-morning air touched at her face and hands, but her cloak kept her warm. She lifted off the balcony and settled in the garden below. She couldn't stop the wide smile from curving her lips as she looked at the thousands of roses that surrounded her. They ran as ground cover, shrubs, climbers, and some were pruned to look like trees. Although it was early spring, the flowers were plump and buds hid amongst the leaves, promising continual blooms. Morgen wondered how they had adapted to the colder Revlin temperatures. Her fingers danced across the velvety petals and serrated leaves, avoiding the thorns, as she wandered the path through the garden. Her boots crunched on the pea gravel as fragrance filled her nose. She cut a plump white rose from a bush with her wand and breathed in the sweet fragrance. With her eyes closed, she lifted her face to the sunshine and managed to find a small chasm of happiness.

"It is beautiful here, is it not?"

She opened her eyes and saw Prince Stephen stand before her. "Your Royal Highness." She dropped into a curtsey.

He bowed curtly before taking a step closer. "That is my mother's rose."

Morgen looked down at the flower and twirled it, watching the petals open a little more. "It is beautiful." She looked up at him. "As is the queen."

Stephen nodded in thanks. He shifted his weight from foot to foot. He seemed nervous, which intrigued her.

"Is there something specific you wished to discuss with me?"

Relief flooded his face. Apparently, she had guessed correctly at the cause of his discomfort. Stephen straightened his posture and looked somewhere over her shoulder. Morgen was tempted to move into his line of vision, to force him to look her in the eye, but she resisted.

"You will be presented to the kingdom this afternoon on the royal balcony." He paused and shifted to the other foot. "The king will declare you as"—he hesitated—"my intended." He dug into his trouser pocket. "You will wear this." He held out a brilliant pink diamond that winked in a silver setting. The cushion cut made it look plump, with plenty of surfaces to capture the sunlight and sparkle brilliantly. Disappointment coursed through her. Although theirs was an arranged marriage, one based upon an alliance, she had hoped for a more meaningful proposal. In her dreams, she had seen herself in a beautiful garden such as this one and her intended looked at her with eyes filled with love. Emotion would fill his voice as he attempted to tell her how much he loved her. His hand would shake as he held her hand and fitted the ring to her finger. They would kiss to seal their betrothal.

Instead, her betrothed stood with the ring extended toward her, his expression one of duty. She scrutinized his face, but could not find one sign of love. As disappointment flashed through her, she accepted the proffered ring and slipped it onto the third finger of her left hand. "I thank you."

He bowed and disappeared down the path toward the palace. She stood in place and watched him disappear up the terrace stairs. Once he was gone, Morgen held up her hand and scrutinized the ring. It was beautiful and the diamond glinted with promise, but she knew no true emotions were attached to it. The only things the ring represented were empty vows and a lifetime of apathy. Hope was not a part of this ring. Neither was love.

With a sigh, she found the path that led from the garden as the ring weighed heavily on her hand. The roses had lost their appeal. Wishing she hadn't cut the white rose, she tucked it into her belt and walked across the lawn toward the orchard. If she could have run, she would have, but it was not allowed. Walking as quickly as decorum allowed, Morgen made her way through the fruit trees that stood in soldier-straight lines and into the thick forest. Stands of tall pines surrounded her, their scent filling the air with the fresh smell so unique to evergreens. Statues and sculptures were tucked into corners and pockets carved into manicured hedges, surprising her with their presence. Morgen ran her fingertips along the toes of a woman draped in swaths of marble cloth and peered up at her blank stare. She wondered what this statue, this woman, had witnessed in all the years she stood guard in this spot. After contemplating the human figure's features a few minutes longer, Morgen continued to wander the forest. A light breeze sighed through the pine boughs and caressed her cheek. Morgen leaned against the fragrant and warm bark and closed her eyes. Perhaps she could endure this life if she was able to meld into nature and find the balance she always sought from the trees and air.

With a sigh, she pushed away from the tree and continued her circuitous path. Soon, the babbling of a brook caught her attention. Morgen followed the happy sound until she came upon the source of the sound. She grinned at the sight of clear water sluicing over small boulders and turning into frothy foam as it crashed over the obstacles. A picturesque bridge arched over the brook, linking each grassy bank. Morgen walked to the gentle apex of the bridge and rested her forearms on the warm wood railing as she leaned forward to watch the water. With a smile, she remembered a game she learned from Beatrice. The humans called it 'Pooh sticks', or something similar. It was a silly name for a silly game. She giggled softly as she went into the grass to look for twigs. After she found two of similar length and breadth, she returned to the railing and dropped them both into the water. She rushed to the railing behind her and waited for the sticks to appear from under the bridge.

"You win!" She clapped her hands as the twigs continued to follow the current away from her. She stacked her hands on the railing and bent over to rest her chin on her hands. It was an undignified, but comfortable, position. Her elation drained away as she watched the current, knowing she could not stay in this spot forever. Her duty was to be the intended of the royal prince, despite his dislike of her and her own reticence of the match.

With a huff, she straightened and slowly made her way back to the fountain. Knowing she would not be able to navigate her way to her rooms via the corridors, she flew up to her window and alit on the carpet just inside. The temperature in her rooms had not warmed much in her absence, so she left her cloak draped over her shoulders. After a quick glance at the clock and the empty table placed by the window, Morgen conjured a simple luncheon. If the palace had planned to provide her with lunch, it would have been brought to her rooms by now. Considering the hour, it was highly unlikely the meal was on its way.

She couldn't help but feel disappointment as she sat at the small table by the window and ate. She entertained herself by watching the plumes of water pierce the air above the fountain. A clock chimed twice and Morgen glanced at the time in surprise. So much of the day had already passed. She sipped the remainder of the cool tea in her cup and waved her hand over the dishes to vanish them.

Thankful she had cared for her fancy gown in the morning, Morgen attempted to change out of her day frock, but was again stymied by the back seam. She closed the small portion she had opened with a touch from her wand and crossed the sitting room to the door. She listened through the door, but couldn't detect any footfalls in the corridor. Gripping the door knob, she slowly turned the knob as she attempted to be a quiet as possible. The loud click of the latch ricocheted through the silence. With a small giggle at the way she jumped at the sound, Morgen poked her head into the corridor and searched for help. No one was present. She closed the door and pinged Lily, but the housemaid did not respond.

Morgen returned to her bedroom and tried again to open the seam of her gown. No luck. She pinged Lily again and this time received a reply. The little fairy arrived at her door moments later, slightly breathless.

"I am so pleased to see you!"

Lily blushed and followed her into the bedroom.

"I cannot open my seam."

"Allow me." Lily touched her wand down the length of the seam and assisted Morgen out of the day frock and into the fancy gown. Once the back seam was closed, she looked at the housemaid. "Are you skilled with hair?"

"No, Your Highness. I am sorry."

The misery in Lily's expression cut through Morgen's heart. "Do not worry. I can manage my hair. I thank you for your assistance."

Lily curtseyed and backed out of the room. The main door clicked shut as Morgen returned to her dressing table and faced herself in the mirror. After many attempts, she managed to weave her hair into braids on each side of her head and wove the ends into a bun at the nape of her neck. Her former lady's maid would again be so proud! With a grin at her success, Morgen rubbed lightly scented lotion into her hands and polished the pink diamond with a soft cloth. Once done, she stood and turned in a slow circle before the full-length mirror. Her gown was beautiful and her hair was a nice accompaniment to the ribbons and lace. She smiled at her reflection once more before sailing through to the sitting room and out the door. Once in the corridor, which was again empty of anyone else, she guessed her direction and managed to find her way to the grand staircase. Her footfalls were muffled by the thick carpeting and she allowed her hand to glide lightly down the carved balustrade.

On the wide landing, she glanced out the window and saw flags snapping in the breeze. She drew in a deep breath and descended the final flight to the lower floor. Standing on the bottom step, she looked left and right, unsure which direction to take. Thankfully, she spotted a footman walking silently in the shadows of the corridor.

"Excuse me?" She walked in his direction.

The tall, liveried young man turned and bowed. "How may I help you?"

"I am Her Royal Highness Princess Morgen of Meath."

She saw a flash of resentment in his eyes before he bowed again. "Your Highness."

Morgen pulled herself to her full height and stared into the footman's eyes. "Please guide me to the royal balcony. I am expected there by the royal family."

"I am at your service." He led her through several long corridors and through two doors before they reached the royal balcony. The king and queen were already present, as were the princes and the princess royal, whom she had not met.

"Here you are." Queen Claire came toward her with outstretched hands. "I am so pleased to meet you again."

Morgen curtseyed. "Your Majesty."

The queen gave her hands a squeeze. Morgen averted her gaze, unable to bear her scrutiny. "Are you well?"

Before she could answer, a stern man in a black frock coat and gray trousers waved his hands toward the doors leading to the balcony. "If you please, Your Majesties. The presentation was scheduled to begin ten minutes ago."

The king and queen took their positions before the doors and Morgen joined Prince Stephen behind them. The remaining royals brought up the rear. Morgen glanced at them over her shoulder. She peeked at Stephen and saw that his stoic expression matched those of his siblings. Even now, as they were about to step before his people, he stared straight ahead without any acknowledgement in her direction. Morgen barely managed to stifle a sigh as she clasped her hands before her and waited to be motioned forward.

The sounds of cheers and applause met her ears as the doors opened and the king and queen stepped out onto the balcony. They stood at the carved railing for a moment and waved to the fairies that filled the cobbled street and the air before them. After an appropriate wait, Morgen and Stephen were ushered out to join them. Stephen guided her to the right of the monarch and the other royals went to the left of the queen. The balustrade was draped in a crimson and gold cloth with cording and tassels. Morgen waved to the undulating crowd and smiled, although she knew the approval was for the royal family and not her.

Soon the king and queen turned and walked away from the crowd. Morgen heard an audible sound of regret from the crowd. Clearly, the residents of Revlin, and Carlow in general, were very fond of their royals. Once within the corridor, Morgen stood next to Stephen and watched the king and queen walk into the depths of the palace. The younger royals split into several corridors. Morgen looked up at her prince and smiled. Before she could say anything, he bowed and wished her a good evening. Morgen watched him walk away at such a rapid pace it was almost comical. Almost.

Stephen looked back at Princess Morgen as he was about to turn into another corridor. She stood quite alone in that horrible gown. That she didn't care even to have new gowns made in the fashion popular to Carlow dampened his concern for her. She snubbed the family during meals, not arriving or sending her apologies to the dining room, and kept to herself. He had checked and was assured she knew her schedule and where she was expected. This was a conscious decision to isolate herself. Keeping her clothing and hair so completely Meathian, without even the slightest nod to her future in Carlow was a very telling trait. She did not want to be a part of his kingdom. She was to be the queen and made no attempt to reach out to her future subjects.

He let out a frustrated huff of air and turned toward his rooms. He was tied to an obstinate and inferior pseudo-royal from a lesser kingdom. Add her poor manners to the incessant teasing from his younger brothers and even his sister and Stephen's nerves were stretched taut. He had hoped to marry for love, as his parents had, but instead was used to forge an alliance with the barbarians to the west. He didn't know why Meath was so important to Carlow's security. The kingdom was inferior, with a less trained military and bordered only a small section of the Red Caps kingdom. He had asked his father why this union was necessary, but was silenced by a stern look. Stephen knew not to continue pursuing this line of questions after seeing that censorious look. The king may be accessible to his family, and promoted open communication, but, after making a decision, he did not want to be countered. Once he received his father's silent message, he had remained silent while inwardly fuming. He felt like a sacrificial lamb and resented his future being decided without his input.

Stephen paced the length of his sitting room like a caged animal. He had been over this particular train of thought too many times. Ruminating about it would not change what was destined to happen. Not wanting to remain within the palace walls, Stephen threw open a window and flew from the palace into the back gardens. The cool air would help clear his head and spreading his wings had always released his hold on negative thoughts. He dipped around the stone terrace and around the fountain before heading into the wilderness at the side of the lake. He wove through the trees and skimmed the pale green tips of the branches as he flew toward the brook. His favorite spot appeared before him as he emerged from the trees and he landed to the side of the wooden bridge. He walked up the gentle arch over the rambling water and leaned back to stare at the fading light of the sky. This was his favorite spot to think and clear his head.

He placed his hands on the wooden railing and leaned over to watch the current eddy and pool around the partially submerged rocks. A leaf caught his attention as it plunged over a rock into a frothy pool of bubbles. It emerged from underwater a short distance away and continued its journey into the unknown. Stephen watched it as long as he could and then turned and following a meandering path back to the palace. He walked, needing the time to think about his situation. He ignored the fact that it was nearing dinner time and he needed to dress. As he walked past the fountain and up the stairs of the terrace, Stephen wondered if tonight was the night Morgen would appear at the family table. He doubted it.

Morgen sat at her small table by the window and conjured a meal for dinner. The setting sun painted the sky with brilliant oranges and purples until it faded into a glowing gray. Her stomach rumbled even though she had conjured three meals this day alone. Conjured foods did not hold the same nutrients as grown food and her body was rebelling. She would not be able to maintain her health if the palace continued to ignore her basic needs. At least there were books in her rooms. Morgen paged through several of the novels until she found one that captured her imagination. She curled up in the corner of her settee and cocooned herself in a warm blanket. As the evening deepened into night, she read by the light of an oil lamp. When her eyes grew heavy, she turned into her bedroom and readied for bed. Lily came at her ping and helped her out of her gown. The wisp of a girl hung the gown with care as Morgen unpinned her hair and brushed it until her locks glowed.

"Would you like me to brush your gown, Your Royal Highness?"

Morgen smiled at Lily as she shook her head. "I thank you, no. I am sure you are longing for your bed."

Lily departed soon after. Morgen fingered the fabric of the

gown and fluffed the skirts slightly. She would brush it clean in the morning. Tonight, she was too tired and overwhelmed by the day's events to think about performing such a task. Once in bed, she waved her hand to close the drapes over the windows and then those that surrounded the bed. She drew the covers under her chin to ward off the chill and, thankfully, fell asleep within moments of resting her head on the pillow. She dreamed of a long table groaning with succulent food.

The next two days were spent in much the same way. She spent her morning hours brushing her gowns and washing her chemise and underclothes in the bathtub, using conjured soap and water. Once her shoes were cleaned and her gowns satisfactorily prepared for their next wearing, she made her bed and managed the light cleaning needed in her rooms. After a conjured lunch, her afternoons were spent reading and wandering the grounds. The gardens and orchards were extensive and she had ample opportunities to investigate the hidden treasures. At the end of the afternoon, she always returned to the wooden bridge and played at least two games of Pooh Sticks before the cool afternoon temperatures sent her back indoors. In all that time, no one came to her rooms to visit or assist with her transition into Carlow's royal fold. She was thankful for Lily, who managed to find the time to assist her in and out of her gowns every morning and night. Lily continued her offers to care for Morgen's gowns and shoes, but she always declined. Lily had more than enough of her own work while Morgen had little to occupy her time.

The third day after her presentation on the royal balcony, Morgen took her normal afternoon walk. She was waiting for the Pooh Sticks to emerge from under the bridge when a shadow fell across the railing and water. She turned and gasped as she dropped into a curtsey.

"Your Royal Highness."

Prince Stephen gave her a slight bow. "Good afternoon."

Morgen shifted her weight as silence stretched between them. "Was there something in particular you wish to discuss?"

He looked to the side and back to her. When he cleared his throat, but said nothing, she smiled at him as her anxiety increased.

"If you say it right away, it will not be as painful."

Was that the faint glimmer of a smile hovering on his lips?

The prince cleared his throat again and clasped his hands behind his back. "There is—There is a state dinner tonight."

Morgen nodded.

"You are expected to attend."

"Oh." Her voice went up two octaves with her surprise.

"Evening dress, nothing too formal."

She managed to stifle her laughter at the idea her wardrobe included a ballgown. "I shall be presentable. Will you send a footman to guide me through the palace? I do not know the way to the state dining room."

"With pleasure." He bowed again. "I look forward to tonight."

She watched him walk away, knowing there was no meaning behind his words. It would not affect him one way or the other if she appeared at tonight's dinner. Likely, he and his family would prefer that she stay in her rooms. That was clear enough by their behavior since her arrival in this horrible kingdom. If she was a valued guest, she would at least have been provided meals, let alone someone to assist her with dressing or maintaining her rooms. Morgen sighed and glanced back at the water. Her Pooh sticks were long gone.

Morgen was perched carefully on a wing chair in her sitting room when the footman knocked on her door. She was dressed in the same gown she wore on the royal balcony, it being the best dress in her meager wardrobe. Her hair was fashioned in the same braids and bun. She tucked in a stray strand as she crossed the room.

The footman bowed low before her. "If you will follow me, I will guide you to the state dining room."

She nodded and fell into step at his side. He led her through long corridors and down two staircases, the molding and objets d'art becoming more ornate as she progressed through the palace. Finally, he gestured to an extravagant set of double doors, flanked by a pair of liveried footmen. She nodded thanks to her guide and entered the sumptuous room. The ceiling soared high above and was painted with a bucolic country scene. The rich colors set off the bright white medallions that marked the anchor points for the crystal chandeliers. The large crystals that hung from the tiers sent rainbows throughout the room. Two large paintings decorated each side wall, showing additional country scenes that allowed the ceiling and walls to blend together into pleasant harmony. The walls were the same white of the medallions and heavy gilding lined the crown molding at the junction of the walls and ceiling, as well as around the panels that cut the walls into large rectangles. At the far end of the room, a raised platform highlighted a gilded and well-polished pipe organ. The floor was a brilliant crimson with a medallion and square pattern that replicated the ceiling.

The royals stood around the horseshoe-shaped table, which was draped in snowy white linens and set with gold utensils. The chairs were gilt with crimson cushions that matched the carpet.

"Princess Fruhlingsmorgen."

She turned from trying to count the multitude of place settings and curtseyed to the king. "Your Majesty." Her hands shook as every person present turned to stare at her. "Please call me Morgen."

"Princess Morgen. You look beautiful."

"Thank you."

The hiss of whispers slid through the small groupings of guests, but she could not hear what was being said. They did not sound supportive and her imagination went wild as her heart hammered. She worked to ignore those around her and concentrate on the king's words.

"May I present Her Majesty Queen Claire of Carlow?

Morgen curtseyed to the radiant queen. Clear diamonds sparkled at her throat and in her hair, as beautiful a foil to her elegant white gown as that first night in the throne room.

"And here is Prince Stephen."

She watched her intended cross the room. "Your Royal Highness." Her curtsey wobbled a bit as he filled in their small group. He did not reach for her hand or show any pleasure in her presence. In fact, he appeared irritated having to spend time with her instead of the elderly couple across the room. Morgen knew he was at her side because of protocol and nothing more. A tiny sigh escaped her lips as she stood next to her future husband who neither loved nor liked her.

"Are you well, Princess Morgen?" His voice was so quiet she wasn't sure if she imagined his words. A quick glance at his face, his eyes piercing into hers, encouraged her to believe they were real.

"Quite well." She matched her tone to his as she kept her gaze on the king and queen, who had turned their attention to a guest who had joined their group.

Prince Stephen touched her elbow and took a few steps away from the monarchs. Morgen followed his lead, surprised when he stepped closer. When their elbows brushed together, a fissure of lightning coursed through her, shocking her with its presence. She swallowed hard and tried to concentrate on what Prince Stephen was saying.

"At dinner, you will be seated next to Prince Edward and across from Lady O'Conor. Lord O'Conor is a marquess of the realm. He is the king's nephew."

She nodded. "How many will attend tonight's dinner?"

"The table seats one hundred and seventy."

Bile rose in her throat as she looked at the laden table. "That many?"

"We will enjoy four courses. The meal will last exactly one hour and twenty minutes."

"What happens if it goes longer?"

"It will not."

She remained quiet as she tried to accept the rather militaristic schedule of the palace. "Tell me more about Lord and Lady O'Conor, if you please."

Prince Stephen clasped his hands behind his back and continued to stare ahead. He had yet to look upon Morgen. "He fell in love with a commoner and chose marriage to her over his duties to the kingdom. His royal ties were put under a sleeping spell, which was broken last autumn when his daughter blossomed into a Gilded Fairy."

She knew her eyes were round as teacups. "Truly?"

He managed to look at her as he nodded.

"What an incredible story! Am I allowed to discuss it with them?"

"I do not see why not." His gaze had returned to the unknown spot ahead of him. Morgen tried to discern what continued to capture his attention, but all she could see was the display of silver gilt displayed to the side of the dining table.

"Is there anything I should not discuss with you?"

"I beg your pardon?"

She looked toward him and was captured in the depths of his blue eyes. "I would like to know more about you. Is there any topic I should avoid?"

His mouth opened but no sound came forth. A sense of triumph swirled through her at his speechlessness. When she smiled and batted her eyes, a crimson flush edged out of his white collar and crept up his throat. She couldn't contain her grin. At that moment, a gong sounded and the king came to her side.

"May I escort you to your seat?"

Overwhelmed by the distinction, Morgen slipped her hand in the crook of the monarch's arm and walked with him to the head table. She stood by her chair as Prince Stephen escorted the queen to her position a few chairs away from Morgen. As he took his place near his mother and Prince Edward came to stand at the chair next to hers, Morgen focused her attention on the lovely place setting that boasted a name card with her full name written in fancy script. The richness of the table enchanted her.

The golden edges of the white chargers sparkled in the candlelight. A booklet bound with a crimson and white ribbon lay atop the charger and the menu card was set at an angle to the left of the gold forks. Crystal glasses and goblets arched around the place setting. After Queen Claire was seated, a footman stepped forward and pulled out her chair to assist her. He took his place behind her chair for whatever assistance she may require during the meal. Around the table, one hundred and sixty-nine others also were being assisted to their places. The sound of chairs moving and skirts rustling filled the air, followed by the quiet clink of crystal as water was poured and wine decanted.

Morgen smiled and nodded to Prince Edward, who sat to her right. Lady O'Conor was seated at the leg of the horseshoe just after the bend from the head table. Morgen touched the Mulryan coat of arms embroidered on the intricately folded napkin. Everything was perfectly lined up and befitting such a regal event.

Her stomach rumbled when the first course was placed before her. It took all her restraint to keep from digging into the beautifully presented fish with a side of delicate spring vegetables. It had been so long since she had eaten such fulfilling and nourishing food.

By the end of the meat course, she was questioning all she knew of Carlow and the royal court. From their conversation to their manners, this was not how the House of Mulryan and the Kingdom of Carlow was spoken of in Meath. In fact, compared to the fairies that lined the long table, she was the barbarian. She was the illiterate rube. This new information was overwhelming and Morgen's head whirled as she tried to make sense of this kingdom. It was difficult to maintain intelligent conversation with her table companions as she attempted to balance the reality of Carlow with the propaganda she had learned in her childhood.

As she finished the fourth course consisting of succulent fruit, served on lovely porcelain plates, twelve pipers played their way through the room. The queen stood and the guests rose with her. Footmen moved forward to slide chairs away as the women proceeded into an adjoining salon for tea and petit fours. The men, Morgen assumed, would spend time with their port and, for those who chose, cigars.

At the queen's invitation, Morgen sat in a plump armchair at a game table. It was set for whist, a game she detested, but she would smile and play in order to please her future mother-in-law. Lady O'Conor sat in the adjacent chair.

"I detest whist."

Her words made Morgen grin widely and Lady O'Conor looked at her in alarm. "Did you hear me?"

"Yes, and I quite agree with you." Morgen's whisper matched the lovely brunette's.

"I do need to censure my thought better."

"Please do not. It is delightful to be with someone who does not parse every word for political or social gain."

Lady O'Conor nodded. "Yes, you are in a difficult situation. You cannot know who is your true friend and who may be using your position for their own advantage." She paused and tilted her head. "It is the same with my daughter."

"The Gilded?"

Her smile lit up the room. She was obviously proud of her daughter. "Have you heard of her?"

"Of course."

"You must meet her. Will you come to afternoon tea at our home?"

"I would be honored."

"Let us set a date. Are you free in two days' time?"

The thought that she might have an appointment was kind. "I believe so."

"I shall expect you for tea." Lady O'Conor smiled. "Informal. Please wear a comfortable gown, for my son, Bobby—Sir Robert, is likely to be dirty from playing in the garden. I would hate for him to ruin a gown as lovely as this." She reached out and touched a fold of Morgen's skirt. "Oh, excuse me." Lady O'Conor drew back her hand and curled it into a fist in her lap. "I am forever breaking the rules."

Morgen touched her arm. "As am I."

"My daughter, Lady Fern, I cannot bring myself to say Her Exalted Highness Lady Fern the Gilded"—she giggled—"she and I are in protocol classes. My instructor would be mortified."

"I will keep your secret."

"I would hug you if that were allowed."

"I would welcome that." Morgen looked around the room that matched the décor of the state dining room. It was filled with perfectly mannered ladies clustered in small groups. "Perhaps not here."

Lady O'Conor's eyes sparkled as she grinned. Their conversation was cut short by the arrival of two more for the whist table. Lady O'Conor moved to the seat opposite Morgen. She was pleased to be partnered with the refreshingly friendly lady and gladly followed her lead through several hands. They had just won another trick when the atmosphere of the room changed. Morgen looked at Lady O'Conor, who watched the main entrance to the room with widened eyes and pursed lips. She followed her gaze and saw an elderly woman standing just inside the sitting room. Members of the royal family quickly surrounded the regal woman.

"Who is that?"

The two ladies seated at the table stared at her, clearly shocked at her ignorance. Lady O'Conor smiled and leaned forward. "She is the Queen Mother."

Morgen watched as the queen and several princesses paid homage to the elderly lady. She wondered how the rather formidable lady felt as she faced her replacement. With a start, Morgen realized that one day she would be in the same position, for she would be queen and would eventually become queen mother.

"What are you smiling about?" Lady O'Conor had moved back to the adjoining chair after the two other ladies scurried over to express their respect to the new arrival.

She laughed. "Just a rather surreal thought that crossed my mind."

Lady O'Conor looked at the Queen Mother and back to Morgen. "I can imagine." She looked back at the growing group of ladies twittering around the royal. "She is not one for diplomatic conversation. Do not take her words to heart."

Morgen nodded and stood. "I believe it is time for me to meet her."

"May I accompany you?"

Relief flashed through her. "Please."

Morgen held her breath and hoped her palms were not sweating as she curtseyed before the Queen Mother. "Your Majesty."

"So, you are the Meathian."

Startled by the blunt statement, Morgen kept her eyes averted as protocol demanded.

"You are less coarse than I imagined."

She stood mutely before her as Lady O'Conor's presence brought her strength and peace.

"Can you speak?"

Morgen nodded. "Yes, ma'am."

"Hmm." She pursed her lips and stared at Morgen with condescension. "I do hope you will begin to appear in a way that will bring pride our family. As of now"—she looked at Morgen from head to foot with a disapproving expression—"you have a long way to go."

Lady O'Conor's sharp gasp was in strong contrast to the smirks of others standing nearby. Morgen managed to nod to the rude royal and backed away. She was across the room before Lady O'Conor touched her elbow and stepped closer. "Forget tea in two days. You must come to our home tomorrow."

"That sounds wonderful." The idea of escaping the palace to spend time with this warm woman filled Morgen with delight.

"Stay all day, if you wish. We have a wonderful library."

"I would like nothing better than to entrench myself in your books, but I believe I must stay within the palace. I cannot appear to run from her words."

"Yes, I see the wisdom in your plan. Come at tea time tomorrow. If you would like to arrive earlier, just ping me."

"Thank you. Let us plan on four o'clock."

"Not a minute later."

Morgen grinned as the men arrived in the room. She watched as the king and the princes immediately moved to the queen mother and bowed. Morgen and Lady O'Conor stood side by side as the king and Prince Stephen moved through the room and greeted their guests. She turned to Lady O'Conor. "Shall we freshen our tea?"

The delightful lady nodded with a thoughtful expression on her face. After busying herself at the lavish tea display, Morgen stood near a window and sipped her tea. Beyond the pane, the moonlight illuminated parts of the garden as others were sent into shadows. Lamplight glistened along the cobbled pathways.

"It is time to say good night."

The closeness of Prince Stephen made her jump slightly. She forced a smile to her face as inwardly she seethed at his command. She drew in a deep breath to calm her heartrate before she turned her attention to Lady O'Conor. "I believe we must leave in order to allow the other guests to return to their homes. It was wonderful to meet with you. I look forward to tomorrow. Please excuse me."

Once in the corridor and away from the eyes and ears of the court, she stopped and turned to face Prince Stephen. "Do not order me around like a servant."

His expression changed to one of surprise. "Did I?"

74

"You did. I may be here due only to the alliance, but that does not lessen my position as a member of your court. It may be unpalatable to you that I am your intended, but that is a matter you should discuss with your monarch. I am merely a pawn in this game of strategy." She lowered her chin and stared directly into his eyes. "As are you."

His eyes widened and his skin pinked. "My apologies, Princess Morgen. I did not mean any offense."

She knew disbelief filled her expression as she arched an eyebrow at him. As her composure began to slip, she curtseyed. "Excuse me. Good night." Lifting her skirts away from her feet, Morgen hurried down the corridor and managed to find the way to her rooms. Once safely inside, she leaned against the door and slid to the floor. Tears flowed freely as the insults of the evening hit their mark. She wanted nothing more than to return to the relative normalcy of her old life, but she wasn't wanted there either. There would be no Beatrice to welcome her and her family would see her only as a hindrance. She was unwelcomed and unwanted in both kingdoms. Her tears fell harder and she buried her face in her hands. Knowing none would come to her door, Morgen did not try to stifle her sobs. She allowed her misery to flow out of her as she released her tight control on her emotions. As she gave in to her misery, Morgen couldn't stop her tears or quiet her sobs.

Her handkerchief became sodden as she continued to cry. Finally, her tears slowed and she hiccupped loudly. Pushing herself to her feet, she slowly crossed the floor. The atrocities of the evening continued to repeat in her head, each slight causing a fresh cut in her fragile psyche. The only bright light was Lady O'Conor. Morgen battled for her sweet voice to sound the loudest in her head. When she could manage a small smile, she pinged Lily for assistance out of her gown. Once the helpful fairy curtseyed and left the suite of rooms, Morgen left her gown puddled on the floor. She shrank her petticoats to a manageable size and slipped them into the armoire before she rubbed the skin that held red marks from the stays of her corset. Wearing her nightgown, she unpinned her hair and cleaned her teeth. As she climbed into her bed, she looked over at her gown and sighed. She refused to subject herself to hours of smoothing the wrinkled skirts, on top of everything else.

Cold air swirled around her feet as she lifted the gown and shook it out. Deep creases marred the back of the fabric, showing her failure to pull the skirts smooth before she sat down. With a frown, she stood with one foot on top of the other in an attempt to warm her icy toes. She would brush and smooth the gown in the morning; she was too cold and tired tonight. With a flick of her fingers, she miniaturized the gown and shook it out before laying it on the long shelf in the armoire. She lifted the layers of her petticoat and frowned at the border of dirt that lined the hem. It needed a good wash, not merely a brushing, but she could never manage their bulk in the bathtub. At least, not as easily as her chemise and other underclothes when she laundered them. She added finding another way to care for her belongings to the already growing list of tasks in her head.

Morgen looked at her canopied bed and frowned. She would not find the comfort of sleep within its embrace. Overwhelmed by the need to escape the palace, she quickly changed into a day gown, eschewing her corset. She was surprised that she could don the gown without assistance. The waist and bodice weren't as tight as the last time she wore it.

Tying on her warm cloak, Morgen flew out the window and to the dense copse of gnarled trees near the brook. She didn't go to the bridge. She didn't want to associate that comforting spot with tonight's debacle. Letting out a sigh, she leaned against the trunk of an ancient oak as the cool night air washed over her. The rough bark pressed uncomfortably against her spine and bit into the back of her head. Morgen didn't care as she replayed Prince Stephen's poor behavior and the caustic words of the Queen Mother in her head. The evening had started out so promising, but all she could recall were their harsh behavior. She closed her eyes as hot tears burned behind her eyelids before they trickled down her face.

"Stupid. Stupid. Stupid." Her words were harsh in the crystalline air. As she continued to wallow in her misery, the sound of a throat clearing sounded from nearby. "Who is there?" She swiped at her wet face as her heart hammered in her chest.

"It is me." Prince Stephen stepped out from the shadow of a tree.

"How long have you been standing there?"

He shrugged. "Not long."

She nodded and dipped into a shallow curtsey. "If you will excuse me."

"You do not—"

"I know." She stomped her foot as her patience disappeared. "Protocol be damned. If I choose to curtsey, then I will. Accept it." She glared at him with her hands on her hips.

"I was going to say you do not have to leave." He held out a handkerchief to her.

Morgen's face burned as she accepted the folded square of fine linen. Unable to look him in the eye, she stared at the toes of her boots that peeped from under her skirts. There was no larger idiot in this kingdom than herself.

"I shall leave in your stead."

She watched his retreating form and pressed the handkerchief to her eyes. "I am sorry."

Prince Stephen stalked through the gardens back to the palace. He had wanted to find some peace amongst the trees; instead he found a weeping princess. A princess he was honor-bound to keep happy and safe. He took the stairs two at a time and went up to the family rooms. His parents had changed from their formal clothing and were seated near the fire, still necessary for warmth during these chilly evenings.

"Son, come sit near me."

He sat on the settee next to his mother and rested his elbows on his knees.

"What is bothering you?"

"She is so—so unwilling to be a part of our kingdom. She is arrogant and snubs us at every turn. Then I see her in the forest. Crying."

"Who, dear?"

"Morgen—Princess Morgen."

"Ah."

He looked at her and frowned. "She looked so miserable. Why? It is due to her own actions that she is isolated."

"Perhaps."

"She has not made any attempt to know us, to know me."

"She is in a new environment. She needs time to adjust."

"How long?"

The queen shrugged. "It is different for each person."

He leaned toward his mother and kept his voice low. "I know it is my duty to marry this girl, but I had hoped to enjoy a union like yours and father's."

She patted his hand. "You have that opportunity."

Stephen shook his head. "We are too different. The only reason we are betrothed is due to the alliance."

"My dear, your father and I were just as separate."

"You married with love in your hearts."

She smiled. "Not for each other. Our love was for our kingdoms and the benefits our union would bring."

He looked at her in surprise. "You were not a love match?"

"Of course not." Her laughter floated on the air, causing several of those close by to turn and smile. She leaned closer to Stephen. "We were brought together for an alliance."

"But you love each other so much now."

"That came with time." She tilted her head and looked into his eyes. "As we learned more about each other, our respect and love grew."

"I had no idea."

She covered his hand with hers. "Learn about her. Show interest in her. Make yourself accessible to her." She patted his hand. "She seems to be an intelligent, beautiful person."

He let out a huff of air and leaned forward again. "I hope so."

Morgen's memory of her meeting with Lady O'Conor buoyed her spirits the next morning She dressed carefully and arranged her hair into a pleasing swirl of braids. Determined to change her habits, she put off brushing and caring for her gown from yesterday's state dinner and stepped out into the corridor. After scrutinizing both directions, she decided to turn right and wandered past several closed doors. Morgen managed to ignore her piqued curiosity and continued down the center of the corridor. When she passed two tall footmen, they kept their eyes averted. Lily was on her knees scrubbing the marble floor that edged the plush carpeting, but did not look up or greet her. Morgen was disappointment, but knew it was against protocol for the housemaid to acknowledge anyone above her station. Morgen stifled a sigh and continued down the corridor.

Near the end, an ornate set of doors with more gilding than the rest captured her interest. This was one door she could not pass by without seeing where it led. She stopped and put her hand on the ornate handle. Before opening the paneled door, she leaned close and tried to hear anything on the other side.

"You are not allowed in there."

Morgen jumped at the sound of the soft voice and released the handle as though burned. "What?"

"This is The Gildeds' Suite."

Morgen looked at the sweetly beautiful young girl standing next to her. She was dressed in a lovely green gown accented with golden fiddlehead fern fronds. Her long auburn hair cascaded down her back in a mass of curls.

"You are a Gilded."

She smiled and nodded. "The newest one." Her eyes were open and honest, without any censure. "I am Fern—Lady Fern."

"Oh!" Morgen dipped into a curtsey. "I met your parents last night. Your mother is wonderful."

Her smile widened. "Isn't she? And you are to come to tea this afternoon?"

She nodded.

"I shall fly with you, if that is agreeable."

"There would be nothing better." She clasped The Gilded's hand tightly between her own. "I am pleased beyond belief."

"I shall meet you by the fountain at ten to four." She paused and cocked her head. "Unless you wish to leave earlier."

Laughter bubbled out of Morgen. "Why would you say that?"

She shrugged and looked at her with wise eyes. "We Gildeds get a sense of things. I sense you are in a difficult situation here in Revlin."

Morgen yearned to confide in her, but remained silent.

"If you need anything, I am but a ping away." She grinned. "I have a very good friend who would like to meet you. Her name is Violet. She is Lady of the Harvest."

Morgen nodded in response to the pride in the fairy's voice, yet she did not know who the Lady of the Harvest was to this kingdom.

"It is a very prestigious position. She is invited to many of the noble homes, as well as events here at the palace. You will undoubtedly cross her path at some point. It may be nice to have already been introduced." She paused. "She will be a good friend to you."

"I look forward to knowing her."

Lady Fern's smile widened. "She cannot come to tea today. May I arrange a meeting soon? She has lovely taste and can help you with your wardrobe."

Morgen's smile faded as she glanced down at her gown. "What is wrong with my attire?"

"Oh, it is lovely." She reached out fingered the ruffle at Morgen's elbow. "I am sure it is the height of style in Meath."

Morgen nodded with understanding. "But not in Carlow."

The Gilded drew in a breath. "Not quite." She paused. "Have I offended you?"

Morgen shook her head. "I assume my hair also is not de rigeur."

Lady Fern circled around to her back. "My mum can help you with that. She is wonderful."

Morgan self-consciously patted her braids. "Will she be"—she drew in a breath— "discreet?"

"Of course." Lady Fern stood before her again and smiled. "I must go inside now. See you at the fountain."

Morgen saw a sliver of a beautifully appointed room when the door opened and Fern slipped inside. The vivacious fairy grinned and waggled her fingers at her before she closed the door. Morgen stared at the closed door for a moment as happiness coursed through her. She had made a friend today. With a smile, she turned and retraced her steps down the hallway. On impulse, she passed by her own door and followed the endless corridor through two sharp turns and several long straightaways. She paused before a tall, arched windows and saw the ornate front gates before her. The presentation balcony must be on the floor below and to the right.

As she considered finding the grand staircase and exploring the floor below, the sound of hushed and angry voices filtered toward her. Morgen glanced about, but could not figure out where the two men were located. A strange shuffling sound accompanied the voices and she recognized it as the slide of feet on stairs. She glanced about but could not find a staircase. Perplexed and unwilling to be caught out by these angry men, she hurried back to her rooms and locked the door.

She leaned against her door and tried to catch her breath. Hurrying such a long distance in a binding corset was not wise. As she waited for her breathing to return to normal, she looked about the safety of her rooms. Perhaps it was not so bad to be confined, instead of out amongst angry strangers. Morgen drew in a final stabilizing breath and returned to the relative comfort of caring for her wardrobe and rooms. She worked through her lunch time, brushing her fancy gown clean, laundering a few small items in her bathtub, and wiping down her sitting room to rid it of any signs of dust. Straightening after cleaning the ornate legs of a side table, Morgen looked about her room and frowned. Her life as a royal princess had become very mundane in this wretched kingdom.

Morgen met Lady Fern at the fountain wearing the same day dress as in the morning, with the same braids in her hair. She could not be anyone other than who she was, at least until she knew how to represent the Kingdom of Carlow instead of Meath.

"Hello." Lady Fern landed to her right with astounding grace. "How was your day?"

She remembered the hours she spent cleaning her rooms and caring for her gowns and clothing. "Busy."

"Yes." She considered her for a moment and Morgen realized The Gilded knew about the lack of assistance in her quarters. It would have been nice for her to offer Morgen some assistance in that respect.

"We are not allowed to interfere with the natural order of things."

She looked at the demure fairy in alarm. Having her private thoughts heard was not something she relished.

"Shall we depart?"

She followed The Gilded into the air and enjoyed tracking the fairy, who was obviously a brilliant flier. Soon she followed her in a spiral down to an impressive stone manor. A tower dominated the union of the two arms of the L-shaped home and an elegant drive curved around the front. They alit on the packed gravel and the front door opened as they ascended the steps under the portico.

"Sean!" Lady Fern enveloped the butler in a hug and he returned her embrace with obvious affection and a wide smile. This was an unusual household. "May I introduce Princess Morgen?"

He bowed low and took her cloak. "The Lord and Lady are in the Rose Room."

"Thank you."

Lady Fern slipped her arm through Morgen's and led her down the lovely corridor.

"You have a beautiful home."

"We have lived here only a few months. I miss our cottage something fierce, but this place has its perks."

"I can imagine."

Lord and Lady O'Conor were seated at a gaming table with an adorable little boy when they entered the sitting room.

"Hi, Fern." The boy waved and took a big bite of a sparkly cookie.

"Hi, Bobby."

"You're supposed to call me Robert now." His words were muffled by the cookie that was still in his mouth. Lady O'Conor admonished him but the sparkle in her eyes belied her stern tone. She wiped his mouth with a colorful napkin and helped him from the stack of books on the chair that raised him to table height. After they cross the room and the necessary formalities were out of the way, Lord O'Conor excused himself.

Bobby—Robert hurled himself at Morgen and hugged her knees through her skirts. "You're nice." She smiled at his cheery face. He grinned back and then looked at his mother. "May I go play?" Lady O'Conor nodded and he scampered from the room.

The next several hours were spent in pleasant conversation and highlighted by an excellent tea. Morgen savored the tasty scones and finger sandwiches, exclaiming over their quality. She deflected remarks that compared them to those served at the palace. She had no experience with the cooking and baking of the royal kitchens, aside from the state dinner, but did not want to disclose the oversight to loyal subjects. They should not know how neglectful the palace was to the future king's bride.

Their goodbyes were filled with hugs, well-wishes, and promises of a quick return to the manor. Morgen's heart was full of warmth and acceptance as she flew back to the palace. She went in through her window and alit on the floral-edged carpet. With a smile, she twirled and hugged herself. It was a wonderful feeling to find friends who accepted her for herself, not for who they wanted her to be. Lady O'Conor had advised her on Carlowian hair fashion. Morgen looked forward the trying some of the hairstyles, which did not involve any braids or full up-dos. Unable to keep the smile from her face, Morgen stepped out of her gown and petticoats and pulled on her nightgown and robe. She unbraided her hair and she began to add some curls when a knock sounded at her door.

"Who is it?"

"It is I, Stephen."

She ran her fingers through her hair as she crossed the floor. His eyes widened as she opened the door.

"May I come in?"

She stepped back without a word, leaving the door slightly ajar as he walked into the sitting room for propriety's sake.

"You look different."

She looked at him in silence for a moment. "I do not know if I should thank you or defend myself."

His eyebrow arched in questions but he remained silent. Morgen was shocked at her outburst. It was unseemly to speak to the crowned prince in such a manner.

"Please forgive me. I did not mean to say such a thing."

He shook his head as if to dismiss her outburst, but continue to stand silently with his hands clasped behind his back. Morgen cast about for a topic of conversation. It would not do to stand looking at each other in silence.

"Were you wanting something?"

He leveled his piercing blue gaze at her. "You missed your appointment today."

"What appointment?"

"The dressmaker, Mrs. Henson, arrived at four-thirty and you were not to be found."

"I was having tea with Lady O'Conor." She stopped and stared at him. "I did not know of the appointment with the dressmaker."

He let out a curt harrumph. "Your secretary should have reminded you."

"I have no secretary."

"Of course, you do."

She straightened her spine even more and looked him in the eye. "I have no secretary."

His eyes narrowed. "You are to have a secretary."

Anger boiled within her. "I am also to have a lady's maid and a chambermaid to assist with my rooms. Perhaps they are with the secretary you presume is in my employment."

"You do not—" The muscles in his jaw twitched as he stared at her and then looked around him. "Who has cared for this room if you have no maid?"

"I am not completely helpless."

He pointed to the cold fireplace. "What of your fire?"

"I have no way to make one."

Stephen whipped his head around to stare at her. "The days and nights are frigid."

"I cannot argue with you on that point." She put her hands on her hips. "However, I had no access to logs or peat, whichever is in use here in the palace. Nor kindling or matches. What would you suggest?"

His face grew red. "What of your meals? You have not joined us at the family table. Who has brought you plates from the kitchen?"

"I conjured my own meals. I did not know I was expected at the family table."

"Conjured?" His lips compressed into a narrow line. "I had wondered why—"

"What?" Her demand filled the empty air after his voice trailed away.

He cleared his throat and looked away. "Your gowns hang loosely upon your figure. I had wondered why they were so ill-fitting."

She gripped the loose fabric at her waist. It was true. None of her gowns fit properly now. She did not need a corset to cinch her waist for the gowns to fit. She could easily twist her gown around to apply her wand tip to the back seam.

"Allow me to clarify." His tone was angry and clipped. "Since your arrival you have not had any meals from the kitchens."

"Aside from the state dinner, no."

"Nor have you had any assistance with your wardrobe, your hair, or the cleaning of your chambers. Nothing."

She bowed her head. "I have the assistance of a housemaid when I need assistance."

"A housemaid?"

She nodded.

"You do not have a dedicated lady's maid?"

"No, Your Royal Highness."

"Your hands are reddened and chapped."

Morgen hid them in the folds of her dressing gown as tears clogged her throat. "I brought a meager wardrobe. I do what I must to keep my belongings clean."

"Explain."

She looked toward the windows and swallowed her tears. "I must launder my—underclothing—at night."

His hands clenched into fists. Morgen shifted her stance for the expected blow. "Where?"

"In the bathtub. I did not know where the proper room was located within the palace."

"You should not be laundering your own clothes."

She turned from his harsh tone and took the chance to step away from him. "What was my option?"

He strode across the room to the windows. "I had been assured these things were in place. Are you sure you have had no assistance?"

Morgen could not stop the laughter that bubbled from her. "I would not have spent hours each day cleaning my rooms and smoothing my gowns if I had help." The dark expression on the prince's face took away her mirth. "I would not have missed an appointment had I known of it." She folded her arms across her chest. "I am not ignorant of my needs for a dressmaker."

He nodded and crossed the room to stand before her. "I must apologize to you. This was a serious oversight and one that will be rectified immediately."

Morgen nodded.

"A lady's maid will arrive at your door shortly."

"May I ask a favor?"

He bowed slightly.

"The housemaid who has been assisting me, her name is Lily, has been a wonderful help and is discreet. I would like her elevated to become my lady's maid."

"She will not know her duties."

"I have confidence she will learn them quickly." Morgen took the chance to place her hand on the prince's arm. "Please." She paused and looked in his eyes. "There have not been many friendly faces here. Allow me this privilege."

Stephen nodded. "You will have her." He looked down at her hand, which remained on his arm. As she began to withdraw it, he covered it with his own and held it in place. "Is this only due to the laundering chores?"

She bit her lower lip. "Your kingdom is colder than I am used to and have no gloves."

Concern flared in his eyes.

"I was advised to bring only the minimum."

He flicked out his hand and opened his palm. A pair of dark leather gloves materialized on his open palm. "Here is a pair of mine. They will be too large—"

She took the proffered gloves and smiled at him. "Thank you."

He nodded. "Accept my apologies regarding this oversight." He paused and gripped her hand. "And accept my apologies for leaving you alone all these days. It was not well done of me."

She withdrew her hand from his. "Thank you."

He bowed and crossed the room to her door. "I will send Lily up immediately to assist you."

"I do not require any services tonight. I would appreciate her help in the morning."

"It shall be done. You will have a warm fire as well. I shall be at your door to escort you to breakfast. It is normally served at nine o'clock. Is that acceptable to you?"

She smiled. "I am usually ready for the day by seven."

"You are up so early?"

"Early morning is the best part of the day."

He returned her smile. "I agree."

"The crowned prince is up with the sun?"

Stephen cocked his head and considered her. "What have you heard about my character?"

She smiled in response. "I'm afraid all my knowledge comes from Meath."

"It is not complimentary?"

Morgen pressed her lips together, unsure what she should

divulge. After a moment's consideration, she decided to remain circumspect. "I'm too much of a lady to repeat what I know."

"Ah, well played." He bowed to her. "Then we must learn about each other without input from others."

"I think that would be best."

"I look forward to it." He bowed again and left her rooms.

Morgen waited until the door clicked shut before she allowed herself to smile. She turned and pointed to the fireplace. "You will soon serve your purpose!" She laughed aloud as she imagined a warm chamber in the morning. Pure decadence!

She twirled through the room and finished her preparations for bed. With a laugh, she realized how early it was and returned to the armoire for a day gown. It slipped over her head and she applied her wand to the back seam. "Last time for that." She grinned as she slid her wand back into the pocket of air at her side and stepped into her boots. Once her cloak was clasped securely, she slipped on Stephen's gloves and flew out to the bridge over the babbling brook.

She leaned on the railing and watched the brilliant moonlight dance on the rough surface of the water.

"Hello."

She jumped and let out a quiet shriek, then laughed at her reaction. "Hello, Your Royal Highness."

"Stephen. Okay?"

"Okay."

"How do you happen to be here? I thought you were turning in for the night."

Morgen shrugged. "It was not time for sleep when you left my rooms."

He colored and glanced over his shoulder. "Please, Princess Morgen."

She stifled a laugh at his sincere, and mortified, expression. "I apologize. I did not intend to have our conversation sound indecent." She looked past his shoulder into the shadows. "His Royal Highness did not make any untoward advances toward my person in my rooms." Her raised voice sank into the darkness.

"I did not mean to imply—"

She laughed. "Yes, you did."

He stared at her from under his eyebrows, which made his eyes dark and brooding, but a smile played at the corners of his mouth. "You enjoy making assumptions about me."

"Do I?"

"It appears so."

As she continued to smile, he tilted his face toward her and the moonlight illuminated his features. He truly was a handsome man.

Morgen reached out to touch his arm. "I apologize, sir, for my presumptions. I should not have believed what I was told."

"You had no other information." He leaned against the handrail next to her and looked down at the water.

Morgen turned away from him and leaned back against the railing. After a long moment of silence, he turned and looked at her.

"You were right in surmising that I do not want to be a part of this alliance."

Her heart thumped dully in her chest.

"However, I am committed to this, to us." He let out a huff of air.

Morgen's levity faded, but she kept her smile plastered on her face.

"I want this to work. It would be intolerable to be committed to someone, to you, for a lifetime without some level of companionship." He scrutinized her. "Do you agree?"

She looked at him and then down at the boards under her feet. "What you say makes sense, but it certainly does not fulfill the dreams I have had since I was a little girl."

"What dreams were those?"

"To finally be part of a family who loved me."

"Finally?"

She shrugged and turned away from the prince. As she stared at the trees, Stephen quietly cleared his throat.

"You do not have a good relationship with your family?"

Morgen kept her gaze averted as she shook her head.

"Does your father value you?"

She shook her head again. Stephen let out a harsh breath.

"Are you the only daughter of King Tobin of Meath?"

She nodded. "Yes."

"Was he reluctant to let you go?"

"No."

When he touched her elbow, she looked up at him.

"Then, why did he offer you in the alliance between our kingdoms?"

Morgen looked away, unable to face him, and shrugged. Emotions swirled through her and she drew in a stuttered breath.

Stephen considered her for a moment. "If King Tobin did not offer anything he valued, how can we trust the alliance?"

The air she drew into her lungs felt like a swarm of bees stinging her lungs. "I do not think you should."

He turned away from her and looked down at the water again. Morgen's chest constricted and her vision blurred with tears.

"I am sorry." She walked to the end of the bridge. "I will not hold you to the engagement." She rose into the air and flew to her rooms as tears streamed from her eyes. She may not love the prince, but she had wanted to find solace in his kingdom. Now, she was without a kingdom and a home.

Chapter Four

Stephen watched her fly away as gloom settled over him like a cloak. Her admission of the poor quality of the alliance sent him into a spiral. There was no good foundation for their marriage now. He could easily terminate their engagement, but the idea caused a sharp pain to stab through his chest. The feeling surprised him. He didn't think the idea of severing himself from her would cause more than a fleeting emotion of remorse. But this feeling, it was different, sharper. It was as though something was being carved out of him.

He turned to stare down at the water again as he thought about Morgen. She intrigued him. He was strong enough to admit that.

He could also admit he had never met anyone like her. She was beautiful and soft, but could be as strong as a willow branch. That was proven by the way she adapted to her sparse life after arriving at the palace. He grimaced at the poor welcome she had received, but it showed she would bend but never break under adversity. He greatly admired that quality.

Perhaps they had been too hasty in their decision to end their engagement. Stephen paused. In retrospect, he hadn't agreed to the decision. Morgen had been the one to suggest it, and had assumed it to be the next logical step. He frowned and turned to look toward the palace. He had not spent much time with her, well, any time aside from the state dinner. From day one she had not been treated as a valued guest. Knowing what he did now of her low status in her father's court, she had probably expected nothing more. He looked down at his hands. It would solve his problem of being forced to marry a stranger, yet there was something about her that made him want to know her more. That would take time. A light glowed in her windows and brought out a desire to know her better.

Without another thought, Stephen flew through the orchard and over the fountain. He landed softly on the small balcony outside her sitting room. He drew deeper into the shadows as she passed by holding a dark valise, the strap and buckle hanging open. Once she disappeared from view through the doorway to her bedroom, he motioned toward the window. It opened easily. She had not locked her windows. He remained standing on the balcony and spoke when she passed by again.

"You do not need to leave."

She gasped and whirled to face him. "Stephen!"

Her use of his given name warmed him. "Do not leave."

"I must. We both know there is no reason for me to stay. I am not to be your bride."

The sadness that tinged her words caused a knot to form in his stomach and he took a step closer to her. "Perhaps we should not be so hasty in our decision."

Morgen placed the valise on the seat of the little chair next to the window. "Do you wish to continue to honor the alliance, knowing what you do of my father's temperament?"

He looked away from her piercing gaze. "I do not trust that your father will uphold his part in the agreement. I do, however, think we should uphold ours. Carlow is a kingdom of honor."

"I would defend my own kingdom, but I cannot."

Stephen held his hand out to her. "Come sit with me."

Without hesitation, she placed her hand in his and stepped through the window. He curled his fingers around her hand as he assisted her, relishing her warmth. He led her to the small wrought iron chairs and table on the balcony. "It is cold. Would you like your cloak?"

With a nod, she called her cloak and it settled around her shoulders. He conjured a hot water bottle wrapped in a foot muff. Morgen smiled when she saw it and lifted her feet for him to slip it into place. "Thank you."

He nodded and watched as his gloves appeared on her lap.

"I thank you for these." She slipped them on and hid her hands under the cloak again. Her appreciation warmed him. He waited for her to speak again. When she did, her eyes and expression were serious. "My father will not back Carlow if it will cost him anything. The sacrifice of his daughter did not affect him, but he will guard his treasury fiercely."

Stephen rested his elbows on his knees and peered at her. "Why is he so willing to let you go?"

She turned her gaze away and shrugged as emotions played across her features.

"Tell me."

Her chin trembled and she drew in a shaky breath. "My mother died. I killed her."

He sat back, not believing that this gentle and sensitive creature could hurt anyone, let alone kill them. "How?" The whispered word sounded like a shout in the still air.

"She died during my birth, or soon thereafter. It was because of me."

"You were a babe. You are not responsible for that."

"I am. That has been drilled into me since my first memory." She looked from her lap to him.

He wanted to reach for her hand and erase the pain in her eyes, but knew his touch would not alter her sadness. "I will argue that point until my last breath."

She looked at him with wide eyes. "Do not let your honor keep you tied to the likes of me. I plan to disappear and bear blame of the broken alliance alone. Your people will not expect anything less of a Meathian, let alone a princess of that kingdom."

"Why are you so willing to take on that burden?"

She shrugged. "Why not?"

"It is something you have always done, taken on burdens not meant for you." He said it as a statement, which brooked no denial on her part. "I will not disengage myself from you. You are my intended and will remain so as long as we both desire the union."

"I do not desire it."

"Look me in the eye and say that."

Her eyes remained downcast. "I am not worthy of your loyalty."

Stephen's protectiveness roared to life. This beautiful girl had been so emotionally beaten she could not see her own worth. She had shown him her strength, which increased his desire to know her better. "You are." This time he reached for her hand, removing the glove before lacing his fingers with hers.

"Please, let me go." She did not try to pull her hand away from his. In fact, her grip tightened ever so slightly.

"If I lost all my senses and let you go, where would that place be? Back to Meath?"

She shook her head. "I cannot go back to my father." She looked toward the garden. "I cannot stay here." Morgen looked at him and he sank into her sad eyes. The slight glimmer of tears tugged at his heart. "Perhaps I will go to another kingdom. No one would know me there. Or perhaps I will stow away on a human conveyance and travel across the sea to the old country."

He shook his head. "You will stay with me."

A crystalline tear slipped down her cheek. "Morgen." He reached out and traced the wet path on her skin. "You are worth so much more than you realize." When she tried to argue, he stood. "Come with me."

She looked up at him, but did not rise from her chair. "Where?"

"It does not matter. Just come with me." He tugged on her arm. "Trust me."

Morgen stood and looked into her sitting room. "My valise?"

"Leave it."

After a moment's pause, she nodded. He tugged the glove back on her hand and then gripped it firmly as they rose into the night sky. Starlight shimmered and the moonlight illuminated the ground passing under them. Stephen allowed a faint smile to cross his lips as the city slipped away and they skimmed the treetops. When a cold draft slipped around them, Stephen began to circle toward the ground. They had arrived at the place he knew would help her see how important she was to Carlow—and to him. When they touched down, he illuminated the empty field with several large balls of light.

"Why are we here?"

He looked at her as his own emotions began to take hold. "What do you see?"

She shrugged and looked around as the balls of light began to fade. "A field, trees surrounding it. Very remote from the city, from the palace."

He nodded. "This is where we fought the Red Caps and gnomes."

She drew in a sharp breath and looked around. "Here? But it is so beautiful. Tranquil."

"It was neither of those things that night." Memories flashed in his mind as he took a few steps away from her.

"You were there?"

He nodded.

"It must have been terrible. The stories I heard—"

"It was worse than anything you may have heard."

Morgen closed the distance between them and gripped his hand. "You must have feared for your life, as well as those of your brothers."

"They were not a part of the battle."

"Only you? Why?"

He released her hand and walked away from her again. He had brought her here to show her how important the alliance was to his kingdom. Instead, he was immersed in his own memories and the anxiety they always produced.

She came up beside him and put her hand on his shoulder. Her touch eased some of his apprehension. "Won't you tell me?"

He turned to face her and saw solace in her eyes. Taking a deep breath, he pushed away his reluctance to discuss that horrible night. "I am the heir. I must show the kingdom that I am a leader. The spare, my brother Edward, must be kept safe. He will lead if I am killed."

Her gasp cut through the night air. "They were willing to let you die?"

"Of course." He looked at her with a wry smile. "Carlow comes first. Is it not the same in Meath?"

"I suppose." She looked up at him and Stephen lost himself in her gaze. "I do not like the thought of you in battle. The danger—" She shuddered and looked about the battlefield again.

Her concern warmed him. He resisted the urge to hold her hand again and pointed to a tree-lined area not far away. "There is where our border was breached." She looked in the direction. "It is also where we sent them back to their realm."

When Morgen took a few steps toward the border, terror coursed through him and he grabbed her arm. "Do not go any further." He pulled her back to safety. "The closer you get to that area, the more vulnerable you become." He walked backward with her in tow. "Do not take the risk."

She followed him without question. "That night must have been so traumatic."

Stephen's anxiety lessened as she spoke.

"The stress must have been overwhelming." She paused. "Tell me how you were able to send them away from Revlin. Out of Carlow."

The fear that gripped him slipped away and he smiled. "It was all due to The Gilded Fairies. Especially Her Exalted Highness Lady Fern the Gilded. She called her Gilded sisters to the

104

battlefield and they caused enough of a disturbance to give us the upper hand."

"Lady Fern? The one I had tea with today?"

He chuckled. "You would not have guess it, would you?"

"No. She is so young and reserved."

"She is, but she has the heart of a warrior."

Morgen looked around the field again. "I can imagine this is now one of the most secure areas of the kingdom."

He looked toward the border. "I had not considered that."

"You have a team that monitors your protective force field?"

"We have a Border Council."

"They have hardened this portion?" She grinned at his silence. "You will not answer?"

He looked away. "I cannot."

"Because you consider me the enemy?"

He drew in a deep breath as the conversation went in an uncomfortable direction. "You are not the enemy."

"But I am not a Carlowian."

He flicked his glance at her but was unable to hold her gaze. He reached for her hand but she stepped out of reach.

"No matter your words, you do not trust me."

"I do not trust anyone."

This time he held her gaze as she studied him. The hurt he saw in her expression cut him deeply.

"I am superfluous." Her words were said quietly and wafted toward him.

"You are not." He came up behind her but kept his hands at his sides and walked with her as she wandered the field. "Never."

"I am. I was in Meath and I am here in Carlow."

He longed to reach out for her, but instead he put his hands on his hips. "I do not want you to feel that way. I am sorry you were unattended since your arrival. I told you of my remorse. I gave you my apology. My kingdom's treatment of you was unforgivable."

"It does not matter."

He stopped and placed his hands on her shoulders to turn her gently to face him. "It matters to me. You deserve better."

Her smile was soft and sad. "You may feel that way, but it does not mean everyone thinks the same. My neglect was orchestrated by someone."

He nodded.

"Likely it was someone within the royal household."

Stephen realized the truth behind her words. He attempted to reassure her, but she spoke before he could form words.

"Until the person responsible is discovered, I am not safe."

Stephen resisted his desire to pull her into an embrace and instead tightened his hold on her shoulders. "I will ensure your safety."

"You cannot." She stepped back and broke their eye contact. Reluctantly, Stephen released her shoulders and did not try to touch her again. "I will leave the palace." When he opened his mouth to argue, she shook her head. "You cannot change my mind. I must protect myself."

"I want you to stay."

She rose in the air. "Announce what you will about our engagement."

When Stephen began to rise into the air, she held her hand before her to stop him. "No, do not follow me."

He returned to the ground and watched her fly away, taking a piece of his heart with her.

"He didn't say anything?"

Lady Fern's use of a contraction startled Morgen and she shrugged at The Gilded's offense to Stephen's actions.

"I kept him from joining me. I needed to be alone."

Lady Fern leapt up from her upholstered chair and her wings snapped in the air. "And he listened to you? I am going to the palace right now to give him a piece of my mind."

"Please do not." She held out her hand to stop her. It was the same gesture she used against Stephen. "He does not know where I am."

Fern plopped back down in the chair. "You did not let him know where you were going?"

She shook her head. "It was not until you pinged your mother's invitation to be your family's guest that I knew where I would stay." Morgen leaned toward The Gilded. "How did you know I needed to come here?"

Lady Fern grinned. "It is the Gilded way."

"But you are not supposed to interfere."

She shrugged as her grin widened. "I can be very forgetful."

Morgen laughed. "That is quite a convenient skill."

Lady O'Conor entered the room with little Robert, who ran to Morgen and jumped into her lap. "Hi, Princess Morgen."

She gave him a squeeze. When his little arms wrapped around her neck, she closed her eyes and smiled. "You are just what I need. How are you?"

"Do you wanna play checkers?"

"Bobby, use full words."

He looked back at his mother and then screwed up his face as he stared at Morgen. "Do you wanna to play checkers?"

She grinned. "I would love to play with you."

Lady O'Conor swept him off Morgen's lap and he went running across the room. "You can say no."

"I am happy to play with him. He is wonderful."

Her face lit up. "I think so, too." When Morgen stood to join Bobby at the gaming table, Lady O'Conor pulled her into an embrace. Morgen stood stiffly for a moment until the warmth of the hug seeped within her.

"Thank you." Morgen's voice was muffled by Lady O'Conor's shoulder.

She tightened her embrace. "You are a wonderful person. I am so glad you have come to stay with us."

Morgen nodded against her shoulder and closed her eyes as tears burned and threatened to fall. It had been a long time since she had been embraced so fully. Her tension eased and she sank into Lady O'Conor's arms a little more.

"Morgen." There was a tug at her skirts. "I mean, Princess Morgen." The tugging continued. She looked down and saw Bobby's big eyes staring up at her. "It is all set up." He pointed proudly to the game table.

She managed a smile and stepped out of the warm embrace. Bobby grabbed her hand and tugged her across the room. Lady O'Conor looked on as Morgen spent the next half-hour playing checkers with Bobby. When the little boy stifled a yawn, his mother stroked his hair and suggested bed. With droopy eyes, he slid from his chair and came to Morgen's side.

"Good night, Princess Morgen." She bent down and he wrapped his arms around her neck.

"I shall see you in the morning."

He smiled and ran from the room.

Lady O'Conor followed him, but stopped and looked over her shoulder to Morgen. "I will return after our bedtime story. It will be about twenty minutes."

Morgen nodded and cleaned up the game and the pile of books from Bobby's chair. He was so small, so young, that he was not tall enough to see a game placed on the table top. She wondered why the O'Conors did not commission a special chair for him. She paused and remembered they had been a family on the outskirts in a small cottage with little of their own. Perhaps they were used to making do with what they had.

Once things were tidy, she wandered about the room. She

stopped when she reached the doors to the back terrace. Without a second thought, she went into the garden and surrounded herself with the cold night air and the scents of flowers and grasses. It reminded her of the time she spent with Prince Stephen in the garden. He had been so kind but, ultimately, had thrown her away. She sank onto a bench as tears slid down her cheeks. In the end, he was just like everyone else. Morgen buried her face in her hands and allowed herself to cry. No matter where she went, love and caring eluded her. Her tears fell harder as she mourned the abandonment she had suffered at the hands of her father, and the subsequent neglect here in Carlow.

A warm arm slipped around her and she peered through her tears into the kind eyes of Lady O'Conor. Without a word, she pulled Morgen deeper into an embrace. The love that flowed into her was overwhelming and her sobbing increased. Lady O'Conor rocked her from side to side but stayed silent, not asking any questions. She seemed to know that Morgen could not, would not, answer them. Finally, her tears slowed and subsided. She mopped her face with a handkerchief.

"Come." Lady O'Conor held her hand and led her through the garden.

The beds were filled to overflowing with beautiful blossoms and foliage. As they passed by a white-washed arch, Morgen looked closer at the climbing rose.

"That is my rose." From the cherry pink petals to the maroon stamens, it was the Fruhlingsmorgen. "How did it come to be here?" She glanced around and saw several of her rose bushed throughout the garden. "I do not understand."

She smiled. "They arrived when you did."

"Tonight?"

"Some, but others appeared the first day you arrived in Carlow and rode in the carriage through Revlin. They are a celebration of our future queen."

She touched a velvety petal. "Then they should be disappearing soon."

"You are leaving?"

Morgen nodded.

"What of Prince Stephen?"

"He does not want me."

"Are you quite sure?"

"Yes."

"Why?"

"He allowed me to walk away."

"You did ask him to let you leave, did you not?"

Morgen nodded again.

"That he did does not mean he rejects a life with you."

"Yes, it does."

She watched Morgen in silence.

She squirmed under her thoughtful gaze and looked down at the gravel path. "There is no reason for him to continue as my intended."

"There is every reason."

She glanced up and saw the compassion in the lady's eyes. "You give me too much credit."

"You do not give yourself enough." She led Morgen to a table and chairs set under the graceful boughs of a weeping willow. It looked out on a small lake with a white, round, open-aired, and columned building. Steps wrapped around the building and led to a grassy bank. It was lovely. Lady O'Conor waved her hand over the table and a delicate tea set appeared, steam rising from the curved spout of the pot. She poured two cups and handed one to Morgen.

"Thank you." She sipped the aromatic blend and a sense of comfort trickled through her.

Lady O'Conor sipped her own tea and watched her over the rim of her gold edged cup. "Does the prince know you are staying with us?"

Morgen placed her cup carefully on the saucer and kept her gaze on the tiny roses and leaves that decorated the thin porcelain.

"We owe our loyalty and our status to the royal family. We cannot keep such a secret."

She nodded and stood. "I will not compromise your welcome. He will be notified directly." Before she could walk away, Lady O'Conor came to her feet and pulled her into another tight embrace. Morgen could not ignore the warmth of her arms and the love and care that poured into her. Morgen's arms wrapped around her of their own volition and she clung to her. In her arms, she could feel all the support and love she had craved for all of her nineteen years. Not even Beatrice could offer such a feeling of belonging. They stood there for a long while. When they parted, Lady O'Conor smiled and wiped the fresh tears from her cheeks. Morgen wasn't aware she had begun to cry again.

"You are a beloved girl."

Morgen's cheeks heated as she heard words she had longed to have said to her for so long. It was as though Lady O'Conor had read her thoughts.

"You are welcome to stay with us for as long as necessary. Lord O'Conor will use his influence with the palace, if it comes to that."

Morgen nodded, but didn't trust her voice to speak.

"Now, go write a letter to the prince. He deserves to know where you are." She stepped away and her hands trailed down Morgen's arms and lightly held her hand. "It is best to have everything out in the open."

Morgen nodded and crossed the garden to return to her rooms.

"Please invite the prince to tea tomorrow."

She looked back and nodded even as her heart flip-flopped at the thought of seeing Prince Stephen again. Once the note was written, with the invitation contained within, it was sent on its way by Sean, the family's butler. Morgen paced the floor of her room as she awaited an answer. She gasped and took an involuntary step backward when Stephen's face flashed in her mind. She was not used to pings, no matter how commonly they were used here in Carlow. After a brief hesitation, she allowed the contact.

"Hello, Your Royal Highness."

"I am still Stephen to you."

She smiled but did not respond.

"Thank you for the note. Why did you not ping me?"

"I did not want to intrude."

"They are not intrusive."

"They were in my former home."

"I will always welcome contact from you." He paused. "You are at the marquess' home?"

"Yes."

"Why did you not stay at the palace?"

Morgen shrugged. "I do not belong there."

"You are my intended."

"Am I?"

His silence lasted so long she was afraid he had severed their connection. Finally, he replied, "Do you wish to be?"

She did not know how to answer that question. Instead, she hedged. "I would like to know you better."

She imagined his nod in agreement. "Then I shall accept your invitation to tea. Thank you."

"We shall expect you at four o'clock."

"I look forward to seeing you."

"Me, too."

"Good night, Morgen."

Goosebumps broke out on her arms. She smiled. "Good night."

Once their connection was severed, Morgen stood quietly in the room as wisps of his memory surrounded her. A ping could be a very intimate experience. She hugged herself and walked across the room.

Morgen awakened the following morning with an overwhelming sense of anticipation. Eager for the day, she dressed carefully with the assistance of a maid. She declined the pleasant girl's offer to arrange her hair and spent time at her dressing table weaving her hair into a crown of braids. She glanced at her reflection before standing. The image staring back at her looked every inch a Meathian princess. Even though she would not be a part of this kingdom, it was time to look more Carlowian. She undid her braids and pulled her hair back in a style she had seen Lady Fern wear. She attempted to curl the fall of hair as she had seen, but could not do a reasonable job of the style. With a shrug, she stood and left her room. She felt ridiculous.

"Only because it is new." Her voice sounded thunderous in the quiet room. The sensation of hair on her neck and shoulders was odd and distracting. She resisted the urge to return to her dressing table and fuss with her hair.

Lady Fern gasped when she walked into the breakfast room. "Oh, Princess Morgen. You look beautiful."

Lady O'Conor echoed the sentiment. "Your hair looks lovely. I had no idea it was so long and beautiful."

"I believe it needs more curls at the back. I could not reach there easily. Can I borrow your maid for a short while longer?"

Lady O'Conor smiled and turned her around to inspect her hair. "May I help you instead?"

"Oh, you should let her." Lady Fern's voice was enthusiastic. "I told you she was a whiz with hair."

Morgen turned to face Lady O'Conor. "I am sure you have more important things to do. The maid will be fine."

Lady O'Conor placed her hand on Morgen's arm. "It would be my pleasure."

"Yes?"

She nodded.

Morgen smiled and agreed. After breakfast, she walked with Lady O'Conor up to her rooms and allowed the gentle woman to curl and dress her hair further.

Morgen glanced out the window and smoothed her skirts nervously with her palms. She continued to pace the corridor at the top of the stairs as the clock neared four o'clock. Prince Stephen was expected at any moment and she wanted to make an entrance into the sitting room after his arrival. She paused. Perhaps it would appear contrived, something he would see through immediately. She may not know the prince well, but he was intelligent. That had been proven already.

The only sensible thing was to meet him in the sitting room. She was near the bottom of the stairway with Sean opened the front door. Prince Stephen stepped into the foyer and the butler relieved him of his cloak.

"Princess Morgen." He smiled and bowed and she stood frozen on her perch.

She managed to descend the final steps and dipped into a curtsey before him. "Prince Stephen, Your Royal Highness. It is a pleasure to have you here."

His smile broadened. "I am happy to be invited."

His gaze held hers and she couldn't stop her own smile from forming. "Lady O'Conor is waiting." Her voice was slightly breathy as her heartbeat tripled in speed.

Prince Stephen nodded and walked at her side through the manor. Morgen knocked lightly on the appropriate door and waited a moment. The prince brushed against her as he reached around to turn the doorknob. She drew in a quick breath, startled by the fissures of lightning that zapped through her at his touch. He tilted his head to look at her, but didn't straighten up or move his arm. She cleared her throat and took a half-step away even as her heart clamored to remain in the half-embrace. He straightened and pushed the door open.

"After you, Morgen."

Her mouth dropped open at the intimate volume of his words. She pulled herself together as she stepped into the sitting room. The marquess and Lady O'Conor stood near the doors leading to the terrace.

She licked her dry lips and willed herself to have the power of speech. "May I present His Royal Highness Prince Stephen?"

The couple came forward and greeted the prince. Lady O'Conor led them to a cozy arrangement of chairs and poured the tea. The marquess departed soon after and the three conversed quietly.

Morgen could barely concentrate on the thread of the conversation as she listened to the prince's voice and watched him through her lashes.

"Princess Morgen, Lady O'Conor, shall we take a tour of the gardens?"

Lady O'Conor politely declined, claiming tasks within the manor. Morgen nodded and walked with the prince onto the terrace and down the stairs to the neatly trimmed hedges of the formal garden. They were an intimate, if silent, duo as the gravel crunched under their feet.

Finally, Morgen could not tolerate the silence any longer. "Is she not wonderful?"

"Lady O'Conor?"

She nodded.

"She is a very warm person."

His reserved tone piques her curiosity. "But?"

He shrugged. "She is a commoner."

Morgen stopped and as her scalp crawled. "Perhaps she was, but now she is a peer of the realm."

He shook his head. "She remains a commoner. She merely married well."

Her scalp crawled as the warmth she felt for him drained away. "How can you say such a thing? She is a lovely person and better than anyone I met within the palace walls.

"I do not think—"

Morgen interrupted him as her anger rose. "If that is the case, I will always be the vulgar princess from the lesser kingdom to the west."

"You are different."

Her hands clenched and her fingernails dug into her palms. "You are wrong. I am from Meath and that means I am dirt under your kingdom's feet." She took a step away and whirled around to face him again. "I shall always be a filthy Meathian."

"It is different. You will be my wife."

"According to what you just said, that will not make a difference." Morgen drew in a breath and willed her voice to be steady. "If you do not respect me, neither will your kingdom. That is an untenable situation for me."

They had stopped walking. Stephen looked over Morgen's head and let out a very unprincely gush of air. She clasped her hands together.

"This is not going the way I imagined." He directed his gaze at her. "You will be respected because you will be my wife."

"No, I will not." She held up her hand to stop his words. "The only respect I desire is yours and we both know I will never have that. I will not be your wife. I will not stay in Carlow." She turned away. "I will always be an outsider here."

"Morgen—"

She drew up to her full height and drilled her gaze into his. "As we shall be no more than acquaintances, it is Princess Morgen or Your Royal Highness. Choose whichever terminology you prefer, but do not use my given name again. That is reserved for my intimate friends." Her vision clouded with tears as she walked away and up the stairs into the manor.

She passed Lady O'Conor in the corridor, who paused and looked at her with concern. Morgen pressed her handkerchief to her face and rushed to her room. Her heart was broken.

Chapter Five

After a restless night and a somber morning, Morgen made her way down to the breakfast room.

"You look tired." Lady O'Conor's observation was blunt, but filled with concern.

Morgen nodded.

"We did not see you after Prince Stephen's visit. Is there anything you wish to talk over?"

There was nothing she wanted to do more, but she did not want to discuss the prince's heartbreaking beliefs. Instead, she busied herself at the sideboard and filled her plate with a selection of fruit and breads. She wasn't hungry, but she wanted to avoid the lady's scrutiny. Lady O'Conor seemed to sense this and made idle chatter through the meal.

"You should eat something."

Morgen looked at her plate. She had moved things around with her fork and broken the bread into bits, but hadn't eaten a bite. She looked up at Lady O'Conor and forced a smile. "I guess I am not hungry this morning."

She nodded and placed her napkin by her plate. "I have some things to attend to. Please do not hesitate to come to me." When she passed behind Morgen's chair, she lightly gripped her shoulder with a warm hand. "For anything."

Morgen nodded. This lovely fairy's warmth and support was more than she had received by the nobility and royalty of the palace. She compared her welcome here to her reception by the coarse Queen Mother. Lady O'Conor won by a far distance. She was far more regal, gentle, and compassionate than that judgmental royal figure. Morgen sighed. Carlow may be a more sophisticated kingdom than Meath, but it fell far short of her expectations in manners.

Eager to find solace, she walked through the manor and crossed the stone terrace to the gardens. Once down the stairs, she followed the path past the tidy kitchen garden. She rubbed an aromatic leaf with her fingers and smelled the invigorating scent of lemons. Another leaf smelled of chocolate and mint. She picked a sprig and held it to her nose as she continued to wander through the cold, misty air. At the archway that was covered with her rose, she tucked the chocolate mint into her belt and ran her fingers along the serrated edge of a rose leaf. As she considered the exuberant color of her rose, Morgen pulled her wand from the pocket of air at her side. With a flick of her wrist, she changed the cerise roses pure white. That was the color of royalty, of acceptance. Emotions clogged her throat as she leaned her forehead against the archway and closed her eyes.

"Princess Morgen."

She let out a small shriek and whirled around to see Prince Stephen standing in the pathway behind her.

"My apologies."

"Why are you here?" Morgen flushed at her direct question. "Rather, I was not expecting you." She looked at him.

"My visit is unannounced."

She nodded, at a complete loss for words.

"I left some things unsaid yesterday."

"On the contrary. I think you said enough." She turned and walked under the archway. The prince followed her closely but did not reach out to touch her.

"I apologize for sounding so—proud."

She stopped, willing to listen to him. "You did not sound proud." Her voice was quiet as she looked at him. "You sounded righteous." She allowed him to lead her to a bench. He sat next to her, leaving a large gap between them. "You have an extreme view of the classes."

"It is the way of things in Carlow."

"You can change that." When he looked at her, she continued. "You will be king someday. You have the power to direct your kingdom toward a new destination."

"How do you think that will be received by the nobility?"

She allowed a smile. "I imagine they will hate it."

Prince Stephen let out a soft chuckle. "That is putting it mildly. What you are asking is to completely restructure our society."

Morgen paused and drew in a deep breath. The air was filled with the fragrance of a multitude of roses, plus the earthy smells of ferns, soil, and rain. She nodded. "Perhaps I am thinking of a utopian society, something that cannot exist in reality."

"Not completely, but perhaps parts of it are feasible."

His compromise was a surprise.

"As for our conversation yesterday, I understand your point about Lady O'Conor. I apologize."

She was silent for a moment as she contemplated his words. "For your beliefs or for expressing them to me?"

Prince Stephen sighed. "You are being very confrontational." He drew in a breath. "How can we resolve this situation between us?"

"Do you still consider Lady O'Conor a commoner?"

"It is who she is, how she was born. To whom she was born."

"If someone is lucky enough to find another to love, who loves them in return, it does not matter their class or rank. All that matters is that they love each other. Unconditional love surpasses all those rigid class systems set up by close-minded individuals."

124

"The place to which she was born matters. It always matters."

Morgen stared at him in silence for a moment, then rose to her feet and walked away. She could not engage in this circular argument again. She could not change his mind, and he certainly would not change hers. All she could do was turn and walk away.

Stephen appeared at her side and matched her pace after only a few steps. "Why must you walk away from me during a discussion? It is a very bad habit of yours."

She stopped but did not look at him. "If it is the worst of my habits, then I count myself lucky."

"It is not your worst habit."

She gritted her teeth at the insult. "I am sure you have a number of engagements on your calendar today. Do not feel any obligation to remain here."

"I did not mean to insult you."

He put his hand on her arm and she was again disturbed by the jolts of lightning that radiated from his touch. "Yes, you did." She disengaged her arm from his hand. "Lady O'Conor is one of the few to show me any kindness since my arrival in Carlow." Tears crept into her voice and she cleared her throat. "That includes members of your family and your household. I will continue to cultivate her friendship." She looked directly at him. "Unless you can accept her as a part of your social circle, we will likely remain separated on this issue forever."

He gaped at her for a moment and then turned on his heel and returned to the house. Regret grew within Morgen as she watched him leave. She had not behaved well. With a frown, she followed his path into the house and peeked into the foyer. Prince Stephen appeared to have departed. She rushed up the stairs to her room and sat at the writing desk by the window. She penned a short apology to the prince and sealed it with a bit of wax she had borrowed from Lady O'Conor.

She hurried down the stairs in search of Sean and stopped short on the bottom step at the sight of Prince Stephen at the front door with Lord O'Conor.

"Oh!"

He turned toward her and bowed. Morgen shakily stepped down to the floor as she attempted to recover from her shock of seeing him before her.

"Princess Morgen."

She hid the note in her hand, knowing it was impossible to hand it to him. Such an act could be seen as a flirtation that was too forward for someone of her station.

"I did not realize you were still here."

He remained quiet and stared at her. Her heart hammered in her chest as she turned to Lord O'Conor. "May we have a moment, please?"

"Of course." He bowed and retreated down the hall.

Morgen watched him until he disappeared through a door before she turned back to the prince. "Please accept my apology for my poor behavior. I was not myself."

"Something tells me you were completely yourself."

She glanced away and crumpled the note in her fist, gripping it until her fingers ached. "You do not have an accurate portrait of my character. I am afraid I have not handled my transition to your kingdom well."

"We have not made it easy for you."

The stress of the past week caught up with her and tears blurred her vision. She looked at him and saw him reach for her. As she leaned toward his touch, he drew back his hands. He pulled a folded square of linen from his pocket and handed it to her.

"Thank you." She dabbed her eyes and pressed the handkerchief to her mouth as she worked to regain control of her emotions. The linen smelled of clear air and rain. She wiped her eyes again and then held it out to him.

"Please keep it. It appears you shall continue to make use of it."

She turned away slightly and dabbed at the tears that continued to fall. "I apologize."

"No need. Tears can be cleansing. At least, that is what my mother has always said."

"Does she weep a lot?"

He shook his head. "She is generally a happy person, but there are times, she says, when tears are necessary. This is your time."

She shook her head. "It is not." She looked up and into his eyes. "My apologies, both for my current lapse in control and for my earlier outburst. Please accept them."

The prince bowed. "Give my regards to Lord O'Conor." He opened the front door and paused for a moment as his wings emerged. She watched him walk down the steps and out from under the portico. When he disappeared into the midday sky, she closed the door and looked down. The handkerchief was balled up in her hand. She held it to her nose and smelled the clean scent again. It was strangely comforting. She took one last whiff and tucked the handkerchief away in her pocket.

The prince visited the manor each of the following three days and Morgen spent hours with him in the garden, or the sitting room during misty mornings. She made an effort not to walk away from him when he irritated her, which was frequent during their discussions. Once he departed on the third day, Morgen sat with Lady O'Conor in a pretty little room that overlooked a sculpted bed that boasted tidy hedges in an intricate Celtic design.

"I do not understand him."

Lady O'Conor looked at her with a bemused expression. "No?"

"We do not get on at all. He is short-tempered and impatient with me, and I cannot abide his elitist attitude. What business of Lord O'Conor brings him here every day?"

"Business?"

She nodded and shifted in the plush chair. "He says it is business with the marquess that requires his presence here at your home. I am a required visit due to his being here already."

"Is that what he told you?"

"The first part, yes. I surmised the latter."

Her smiled broadened. "My dear, the marquess has no pressing business with the royal prince at this time."

She stared at her.

"You are what brings him here every day."

"Me? I do not understand."

"He is courting you. Did you not know?"

"How could I know?"

She reached over and covered Morgen's hand with hers. "Do not blush so. It is a sweet gesture."

"I do not know what to think." Her heart hammered in her chest. "I feel a bit like a fool."

"Why?"

"I am the object of his private joke. That is cruel."

"I do not believe it is a joke."

"I do." She let out a short breath. "We argue incessantly. I cannot see how we could ever make a happy match." She turned to face her fully. "However, there are times when—"

"Hello!"

Morgen looked over her shoulder at the enthusiastic greeting and saw Lady Fern come across the room with a smile on her face. Lady O'Conor rose and the two embraced. Jealousy flared through Morgen as she coveted their affectionate relationship.

"Good afternoon, Princess Morgen."

She stood and curtseyed. Lady Fern waved her hand. "Please do not observe those formalities here." She pulled Morgen into an embrace. "I am so happy every time I return home and see you here." She released her. "Did you have a nice visit with Prince

Stephen?"

"How do you always know what has happened?"

Her smile widened. "It is the way of The Gildeds." She giggled and her mother joined her. Morgen's irritation returned as she was again the object of someone's joke. "I am sorry. Lady Fern rested her hand on Morgen's arm. "I am not laughing at you."

"What she said, it is something her Gilded mentor always said to her. She would be so angry when Lady Zepherine said the same." Lady O'Conor giggled again. "Now, she is the one saying those words."

"It is the perfect answer." Lady Fern laughed and sat down in a chair near Morgen's. "Tell me everything about his visit."

She lowered herself into her chair.

"Princess Morgen just discovered that she is the cause of Prince Stephen's visits."

Lady Fern smiled at her mother and then turned her attention back to Morgen. "Yes, that would be a surprise. How do you feel about it?"

"I am not sure."

She smiled. "Everything will be for the best in the end."

"Is that secret information from a Gilded?"

She returned Morgen's grin. "Do not tell anyone I told you."

The trio laughed and Morgen's mood lightened.

The strange this is"—she paused—"Prince Stephen said he pinged me every day before he arrived."

"Did he?"

"Not that I can tell."

"Could you have missed it?"

She shook her head. "They are too much of a novelty for me to miss." Morgen looked out the window. "Why would he lie about something so trivial?"

Both ladies defended the prince, which Morgen though was to their credit.

"I remember the same thing happened between myself and Thomas. It was very unsettling." Lady Fern smiled. "Do you remember that, Mum? It was during the Harvest Ball, right before Violet was crowned."

"Thankfully, you were able to discuss it before it caused too much mischief." Lady O'Conor directed her attention to Morgen. "Do not allow a wayward ping to cause unnecessary trouble for you."

"Do they usually go astray?"

"No."

"After the Red Caps and gnomes attacked, we were able to ping. We successfully repelled them in large part because of our ability to send mental messages."

"Perhaps I cannot receive them regularly due to my heritage. Maybe it is a border thing. Since I am not from Carlow, there is some sort of barrier?"

"Perhaps, but I will still mention this to Lord O'Conor."

"Good idea, Mum. Anything different—" Lady Fern's voice trailed away and she had a faraway look in her eyes. Lady

O'Conor delicately cleared her throat. "Sorry." Lady Fern laugh was edged with self-consciousness. She turned her attention back to Morgen. "Did you have any missed pings before you arrived in Carlow?"

"I received pings very little. My governess and I usually spoke whenever we needed to discuss anything. She pinged me when I required assistance with my manners and posture, or when I needed some support during a—discussion—with my father."

"What of your family? They did not ping you?"

She looked at Lady O'Conor. "They rarely had reason to speak to me. When they did, it was through my governess or a written note delivered by a page."

"You were kept very separate, very alone." Lady Fern's voice was quiet, but very focused. "Do you know why?"

"It was simply the way it was." Morgen would not reveal her dark secret to anyone else. It was bad enough that Prince Stephen knew. "I did not know families were any different until I arrived here. To see the king and queen together and consorting with their children was very strange. They appear to enjoy each other's company, as do you. Is that normal behavior throughout Carlow?"

Both ladies nodded. "Family is very important to our kingdom."

"Is that why the prince is pursuing our match? He wants to satisfy his father's desire for the alliance?"

Lady O'Conor tilted her head. "That is something you must ask him."

Morgen looked out the window again and traced the Celtic

hedge with her gaze. It would be difficult to broach the subject with the prince. She was not accustomed to discussing such personal issues with anyone but Beatrice.

Stephen arrived at the O'Conor manor directly at ten o'clock the next morning, as had been requested by Princess Morgen. He stood in the foyer as Sean took his cloak, with his heart hammering in his chest. She had asked for him, which was a generous move in the proper direction. He smiled and followed the butler to the sitting room where he awaited Morgen's arrival. Funny how he had not valued her as much when she lived at the palace and was more accessible. Now, he had to make excuses and false appointments in order to see her. Thankfully, Lord O'Conor had agreed to his plan and followed his lead in the deception of duties that called him to the marquess' home each day.

He sat in a chair, then jumped to his feet and stared out the window as he awaited Morgen's arrival. He was eager to see her, despite their frequent arguments. He enjoyed the debates, learning her opinions, and seeing her passion. He was not afraid to admit that sometimes he purposely took to opposing side simply to provoke her and cause her passion to spill forth.

The sound of the soft knock at the door caused him to grin. He turned eagerly and watched Morgen enter the room and cross the floor toward him.

"Prince Stephen, thank you for coming."

He bowed. "I am at your service."

She gestured toward the back terrace. "Shall we take a turn in the garden?"

He nodded. She was most relaxed in nature and he enjoyed accompanying her along the paths as she exclaimed over colorful flowers and fragrant grasses. If a small animal happened to wander across the path, she was ecstatic. Perhaps then he would take the chance to hold her hand. Stephen hoped for a wee animal and contemplating conjuring a baby rabbit or kitten for her amusement. He offered his arm at the top of the stairs and walked with her to the gravel pathway. The further they ventured into the garden, the more nervous she appeared, yet they continued in silence. As her hand trembled, he took pity on her.

"Was there a particular reason for your invitation this morning?"

Her fingers convulsed on his arm as they continued to walk. She drew in a breath and held it for a moment. He was intrigued.

"Why do you continue to call on me?"

His optimism deflated a bit. "Do you wish me to end my visits?" He hoped she would say no.

Instead, she seemed to skirt the issue. "We had decided the alliance would never be upheld by Meath. There is no reason for your marrying me. My father will not come to the aid of Carlow."

He stopped walking and turned to face her. He held her hands loosely in his. "I discussed your fears with my father. He insists that we honor the alliance."

"Even though it is likely my father will not? Are you sure he understands this?"

Stephen nodded. "He maintains that we must honor our commitment."

"As I am from Meath, and the spawn of a dishonorable king, do you expect that I will behave dishonorably?"

"No." He smiled at her. "You have proven to be very un-Meathian in your behavior."

She withdrew her hand from his. "Is that a compliment or a criticism?"

His brow furrowed as he captured her gaze in his. "It is an observation, that is all. Please do not read anything more into my words."

She looked away. "I am in a difficult situation."

"Please explain."

"I am from Meath and I feel a loyalty to my land, if not my father. Yet, now I see how it is viewed from afar. My initial response is to defend it, no matter how truthful your statement."

He nodded. "Loyalty is a considerable trait."

"I fear it is misplaced."

Stephen lifted her hand to his arm and walked with her down the path. He slowed when he sensed her interest in a flower or a leaf, trying to decide if this was the place for his conjured rabbit to bound across their path. He wanted to draw her close and wrap his arms around her. Instead, he led her back toward the terrace and stopped before she started up the stairs. He didn't want her to leave and thought of a way to keep her at his side, at least for an hour or two longer.

"Come with me."

She looked at him with wide eyes. "Where?"

"I would like to show you a place that is special to me."

"I do not think—"

He grinned at her hesitation. "You are correct. We should have a chaperone."

"Prince Stephen! Princess Morgen!"

He turned to see Lady Fern skipping down the stairs toward them. It was unseemly for such a regal person as a Gilded to skip, yet on her it was completely natural. He grinned at her exuberance and looked down at Morgen. She smiled as well.

"May I ask a favor?" Lady Fern hurried toward them.

He bowed to her.

"I wish to visit my tree. Will you accompany me there? You too, of course." The latter was said to Morgen. Her smile was genuine, but he detected a mischievous glint behind The Gilded's innocent grin.

"I will gladly fly with you. Princess Morgen?"

She looked up at him and nodded.

"Thank you so much. Father and Mum are so busy with their own projects and I am meeting my friends there. May we leave soon?"

Morgen called down the prince's gloves and ensured the clasp was in place on her cloak. "I am prepared."

The sight of his gloves on her hands made Stephen smile. He

called his cloak and, once it was in place, prepared for flight. He followed Lady Fern into the air, making sure Morgen stayed at his side. He admired The Gilded's flying skills, but saw that the princess had difficulty following her quick path. He slowed his pace and pointed out landmarks in the city.

"There is Longford, where I went to school."

Morgen looked down at the imposing stone building and then to him. "You must tell me about it someday."

Her use of 'someday' lightened his heart. "Where were you schooled?"

"At home with my governess." She looked down again. "What was it like to be around all those students?"

He followed her gaze and saw throngs of young fairies scurrying about the courtyards and the front stairs. "It was good, if a little crowded. Sometimes it was not so good."

"When?"

He regaled her with stories of his years at school, causing her to alternately laugh and commiserate. Too soon, they reached the edge of the lake and the tall tree that Lady Fern favored.

"I shall leave you here." Lady Fern hovered near the apex of the tree. "Thomas and Violet have already arrived." He looked and saw the glow of a small fire on the ground under the protection of the tree's boughs. The figures of two fairies waved. He waved back and saw Morgen do the same.

"We shall be there." Stephen gestured down the shoreline. "Ping me when you are ready to leave."

Lady Fern waved and flitted to her friends. Her rapid descent was impressive. He looked at Morgen and saw her pale a bit at The Gilded's flight. "You should see her during a performance."

Morgen looked at him with wide eyes. "I look forward to that."

He considered that another victory. She was speaking of a future in Carlow. Stephen led her a short way along the lake, slowing to a hover so she could admire the impressive waterfall. He pinged her and saw her jump in surprise. "Do you like it?"

She nodded. "Yes."

"When you are ready, we can go to the ground and warm up."

She hovered for a moment more and then slowly lowered to the ground. He conjured a small fire and she stepped closer to its warmth. He watched her for a moment.

"You are not used to a ping, are you?"

She looked at him in surprise. "Why do you ask?"

"Your reaction. You were surprised."

She nodded. "It was a bit—intimate."

"You are not accustomed to such intimacy?"

Fire flared in her eyes. "I am a maid."

He held up his hands and patted the air in supplication. "That was not my meaning. I know you are pure. What I meant to ask was if you were accustomed to an intimate inner circle."

Her breath clouded in the cold midday air. "I was close to my governess."

"What about your family? Your father and brother?"

She shook her head. "Only my governess."

"Tell me about her." He conjured a small padded chair near the fire and indicated it was for her. Another appeared next to it for himself. He supplied her with a foot warmer after she took her seat.

As he waited for her to begin, he brought forth a table with a steaming pot of tea and two teacups. When he reached to pour, she waved his hands away.

"Allow me." Once the tea was poured and she cradled the cup in her hands, she settled into her chair and told him about Beatrice.

"You sound as though you miss her."

"I do. She was a wonderful friend."

"Why did she not come with you?"

"She was needed at home." She sipped her tea. "This is wonderful. Thank you."

"Do you miss your brother?" He leaned on his own brothers something fierce.

"Dougan was kept separate from me and we grew up without knowing each other well."

"Honestly?"

"Yes. The heir should not consort with"—she paused and drew in a breath—"someone such as myself."

Ah, so that is where some of her reticence came from. He placed his cup on the table. "You should not consort with your brother? You are the princess."

"In my kingdom, that does not hold much influence."

"Which is why you say the alliance is made of air."

She nodded.

"What will happen if the Red Caps and gnomes attack Meath?"

"My father will expect Carlow to come to his aid."

"And if they attack Carlow again?"

"You will wait too long for a force that will likely be insufficient."

"You are very blunt."

She shrugged. "You asked for the truth."

"I suppose I did." His enjoyment of their conversation increased with her teasing smile.

"Do you disapprove?"

"Of your direct answer?"

"Yes."

"I am unaccustomed to a princess being so forthright."

A smile ghosted across her lips. "You have been presented to several princesses then?"

"I—I—" He stammered as he searched for an answer.

Laughter burst from her. She tried to swallow it, but it grew until she fairly shook with mirth. She gasped for air. "I am sorry."

He laughed with her. "Do not apologize."

"It feels good to laugh again." She covered her mouth as she tried to regain her composure. "Oh, Prince Stephen, I am so sorry." She cleared her throat, but the sound did not cover her continued giggles.

He chuckled a few more times. "You are the most refreshing princess I have ever met."

"I believe you mean uncouth."

He forced his mirth down and looked deeply into her eyes. "No. Absolutely not."

"Ill-mannered?"

"Definitely not." He arched an eyebrow as she smirked at him. "I find you intriguing."

Her cheeks flushed.

"Life will be interesting with you at my side."

Her expression turned serious. "You still want to marry me?"

He smiled at her. "I believe I do."

"Because you are under orders from your father."

"This goes beyond his edict."

"You *want* to marry me?"

"You already asked that question."

"But it must be asked again. Why would you do it, beyond the desire to please your father?"

He did not tease her, understanding she wanted a serious answer. "I have never wanted a simpering wife, a conformist. I cannot imagine you coming close to that description."

A small smile played on her lips. "I do not believe I would."

He reached over and held one of her hands as he dropped to one knee before her. "Will you agree to marry me?"

She looked at him and then broke their connection to look down. "I do not want to accept your proposal merely because I have nowhere else to go." She stood silently, with her hand in his, and continued to look anywhere but in his eyes. He continued to kneel on the cold ground, hoping she would agree. She had captured his heart, he couldn't say how.

"I am asking for myself. Not for my family or my kingdom." He paused and willed her to look at him. "Just me."

She finally did look at him, scrutinizing him for an eternity. He refused to fidget under her gaze. "Do you consider me inferior because I am from Meath?"

He shook his head. "I thought of your words all last night. You are a wise voice in my head."

"Oh, dear."

Stephen laughed. "It is not a bad thing."

"If you can change, so can I." She tugged him back to his feet.

He stood before her and continued to hold her hand. "Are you going to give me an answer?"

Morgen laughed lightly and gave his hand a squeeze. "I am so sorry." She continued to look deeply into his eyes. "I would be proud to be your wife."

Unable to restrain himself, he pulled her into an embrace. "We will do great things together."

Chapter Six

Morgen walked with Stephen along the lakeshore with her hand on his arm. She embraced the warm glow that surrounded her after his heartfelt proposal. It was like a dream that she remembered longing for since she was a wee girl.

"What are you thinking?"

She grinned. "That you are the answer to my dreams." Her smile deepened as he blushed adorably. "I believe that is your cue to compliment me."

He chuckled at her teasing tone and covered her hand with his. "Then I will tell you that I have always dreamed of a fiancée who is spirited and not at all a shrinking violet."

"Then we shall both be satisfied."

He stopped and turned toward her. "Morgen, would it be too forward of me to kiss you?"

Her heart leaped. "Most likely, but I shall not utter a word."

He smiled and leaned toward her. Morgen held her breath as she waited for the touch of his lips. Just as the warmth of his breath feathered against her cheek, an iron grip pulled her backward. She gasped and called out his name as she continued to be torn away from his promise.

A dark and raw feeling of hopelessness filled her as a curtain of energy dimmed her vision. When a horrible pain tore through her, Morgen realized she had been pulled through the border. She stood in the no-man's land between realms and saw Stephen on the other side of the energy field with a look of terror on his face. When a painful grip forced her to turn away from him, she screamed as abject terror tore through her. Three Red Caps surrounded her. She continued to scream as one reached toward her with long and bony fingers.

"Come." His knit cap was not dripping with bright red blood as normal, but was hardened with the dark brown hue that could be only dried blood.

Morgen pretended not to understand what the Red Cap said, not wanting them to know she spoke their guttural language. She shrank away from his clawing hand and he stepped closer. His grin was tinged with evil as he wrapped his fingers around Morgen's upper arm and pulled her toward the border behind him.

She looked back at Carlow and saw Stephen run at the energy field. He bashed his shoulder into the border again and again without success. Even the crowned prince required consent before passing through the border. Morgen couldn't understand how the Red Caps managed to pull her through.

"Stephen!" Her repeated cries made no difference. The Red Cap's fingers dug deeper into her arm as she tried to pull away from him.

"Just take her."

The Red Cap holding her obeyed the growled words of his companion and pulled Morgen to his side. She gagged at his odor of rotting flesh and tried to pull away from him. He drew her closer. She wrenched at her arm again and tried to jam the hard heel of her boot into his shin and foot. The Red Cap was undeterred and continued to pull Morgen toward the opposite border. She struggled, knowing she would face a terrible fight to stay alive if she crossed into the Red Cap's realm.

Morgen saw Stephen try again to cross the border. "No!" She knew he would never hear her through the border, but she continued to cry out. As the Red Cap dragged her further away from Stephen, she continued to look back at him. He was in a frenzy trying to get through the border. Tears streamed down her face as he threw himself against the border again and again. White hot pain seared through her as the Red Cap border encased her and flowed around her. Her skin felt on fire and it seemed every cell in her body was about to explode. She screamed out as the pain became unbearable.

Just as suddenly, the pain ended and Morgen found herself in a forest similar to that of Carlow. Her head ached and began to swim as the ground rocked under her feet. The trees around her swayed back and forth and her vision tunneled into pinpricks. As her nausea increased, Morgen sank into blissful darkness.

Stephen sank to his knees after he sent an urgent ping to Lady Fern and Sir Thomas. His shoulder throbbed from the multiple beatings against the energy field. Even though he could not see through the border into the no-man's-land, he knew Morgen was there, just beyond his reach. He turned his face toward the sky and yelled his frustration.

"Prince Stephen, what is it?"

He turned to see Lady Fern, Sir Thomas, and Miss Violet fly toward him.

"Red Caps." He stood as he cleared his throat. "They took Morgen."

Their faces paled at his words.

"How?"

He looked at Fern and shook his head. "One reached through our border and grabbed her. I do not know how." He stared at the place where Morgen disappeared. The Red Cap's realm was just beyond that spot. "She is gone."

Fern put her hand on his arm. "Do not lose hope. We will find a way to get her back." She gave his arm a squeeze. "I shall contact my father." She paused. "He isn't answering my pings." Her eyes widened and she looked toward Thomas. Stephen realized the meaning of her words and drew in a sharp breath.

"Just like before the battle." They spoke in unison. Violet gasped.

"It is their tell." Thomas' voice was low and fierce. "Now we know when they are attempting to breach our border."

"When we cannot ping."

"Morgen told me she had not received any of my pings these past few days." He let out an oath and looked at Thomas. "I should have realized—"

Thomas put a hand on his shoulder. "None of us knew what it meant. Do not abuse yourself."

Stephen turned and stared at the border. "We must get her back."

"We will."

"It does not mean anything that we know their tell now. They have her. There is nothing more they can do to me."

Fern's gentle touch was little comfort. "I'll try Dad again." She paused. "Your Highness, how long has it been?"

"About four minutes." He closed his eyes. Four long minutes.

Fern touched his arm again. "The Border Council requests your presence immediately."

Stephen nodded and looked at Thomas. "Convene the knights. We shall need their skills."

Thomas bowed and stepped away. He returned quickly. "My

ping has been received. The Order is gathering and will meet you at the Border Council."

Stephen nodded his approval and looked back at the border. He hoped Morgen was still alive.

The clouds in Morgen's mind cleared and she found herself slung over a Red Cap's shoulder. They were clomping through the forest on a wide dirt trail. One of her arms was pinned between her side and the Red Cap's neck. Her other arm flopped unceremoniously over his shoulder and her nose was smashed against his back. His horrid odor filled her nostrils and she turned her head to gain fresher air.

"She's awake."

At his companion's growled words, the Red Cap carrying Morgen dumped her to the ground. She let out a cry of pain and tried to scramble to her feet. Searing pain coursed through her as one of the Red Caps kicked her in the abdomen. Another clawed at her back, ripping the fabric of her cloak and bodice. She cried out again and pulled her skirts out from under her feet so she could stand. They pushed her to the ground again and kicked her in the ribs. Morgen heard a distinct cracking just before blinding pain coursed through her. Another Red Cap kicked her in the same location in her ribs, causing nausea to course through her.

"Leave her. He wants her to arrive whole."

Morgen had just enough sense to continue pretending she did not understand their language. The two other Red Caps grumbled as she dragged herself to her feet and gripped her cloak around her. She wanted to cry out with every step, but managed to remain silent. Two of the Red Caps flanked her and one walked before them, leading the way through the forest. Each step increased her pain. As they made their way along the rutted trail, the forest gave way to scattered little huts surrounded by yards of packed earth and scrawny trees. There wasn't a flower in sight. Red Caps in various loose and grubby garments watched her pass from their windows and doorways. Hissed words and mean taunts were hurled at her by both adults and children. Sticks and rocks were thrown by the dirty Caps along the road. When they made contact, she refused to cry out. She would not show any sign of weakness, a lesson she learned at the fist of her father. They would have to be satisfied with her blood, which flowed stickily from the fresh injuries.

The dirt trail transitioned into a packed dirt road, lined with more Red Caps eager to see the prisoner. Morgen kept her gaze straight ahead. When she stumbled on a rut, there was a murmur in the crowd. She could imagine their hopes that she would fall. With her skirts clutched beneath the length of her cloak. Morgen managed to remain upright and attempted to walk with dignity. Her resolve faltered as they emerged from between several large buildings and into a large square.

The space was jammed with Red Caps of all genders and ages. Every one of them spewed hatred at Morgen. She drew upon all her strength and managed to walk through their midst without reacting. Those closest clawed at her, their sharp nails piercing the fine wool of her cloak and scraping along her arms, shoulders, and back. Her hair was snagged and torn from her scalp. Morgen wished she had kept her hair twisted up in her normal braids, but she had wanted to impress Stephen.

Stephen! What he must be feeling right now. She tried to ping him, knowing there likely would be no answer. Pings couldn't cross borders, yet she was disappointed all the same. It would be fortifying to hear his voice.

Knowing she must rely on herself, Morgen steeled herself as she approached a pillared building made of dark stone that dominated one side of the square. It was ugly and ominous with angular lines and no windows. One of her captors pushed her toward it. A pedestal was situated halfway up the stairs. It looked like the pedestal that usually held up a statue, except this was empty. Neither stone man nor stone beast topped the block of stone. As she approached, Morgen could see it was more of a plinth. Her scalp crawled. Her only knowledge of a plinth was when it was associated with the ancient form of sacrifice. Was this where they would kill her? She closed her eyes and whispered words of encouragement to herself.

"Get going." She was shoved forward again.

She managed to keep her feet under her as she continued across the square. Her gaze remained glued to the plinth and all too soon she stood in its shadow at the base of the stairs. She drew in a deep breath and willed her hands to stop shaking. The crowd behind her murmured in anticipation. Tears burned in her eyes, yet Morgen held them back. She would not show any weakness.

The Red Cap that carried her through the forest came up behind her with a growl. Morgen whispered Stephen's name as the creature swept her up in one deft movement. Before she realized his intent, he carried her up the stairs and lifted her onto the pedestal. Some unknown force locked her into a seated position with her legs hanging off the edge. Her hands were in her lap and her back was straight as a wand. She faced the square and stared at the mass of Red Caps. Fear coursed through her as she realized her state, paralyzed atop the plinth and unable to move a muscle. Thankfully, she could breathe and blink her eyes, but she couldn't shift in place or move her arms or legs.

She screamed in her head, "Help me!". She tried to plead for mercy but no sound emanated from her throat. As her three captors disappeared into the crowd, the gawking Red Caps pressed forward. Those closest to her reached out with their long and gnarled fingers. Fear ripped through her as their sharp claws sank into her cloak and skirts. More Red Caps pressed forward and tore into the fabric of her clothing, taking shreds away like a prize.

One Red Cap's fingernail cut through the cloak and caught in Morgen's wing. He tore down and away, piercing a jagged rip in the fragile membrane. Somehow, her cry of pain filled the air. She didn't understand that she could cry, but not speak. Understanding washed over her as she realized they wanted to hear her pain. This must be a special spell that gives them the sounds they wanted, but kept her from pleading and speaking.

The crowd cheered and became more zealous in their clawing as she let out another cry. Morgen closed her eyes and though of Stephen as streaks of pain shot through her. She didn't know how much more she could endure before she lost control of her senses.

"I do not blame you for what is happening to me."

She knew her ping would not reach Stephen but she needed to divert her mind from the pain of the Red Caps' claws cutting through the skin of her ankles, calves, and arms. Instead, she remembered the comfort of his touch and the warmth in his eyes. She continued to talk to him, releasing all the feelings in her heart.

"You were forced into this engagement, as I was, and did what you needed in order to delay the inevitable. I would have likely behaved in the same manner if you had been brought to Meath." Tears filled her eyes. She was not sure if they were caused from the pain of her attackers, or from regret that she would never see Stephen again. "I hope you find happiness."

Morgen continued to ping Stephen as blood dripped from her wounds and tears slid down her cheeks. The torment continued for hours. She was lightheaded and struggled to maintain consciousness as the spell she was under kept her locked in a rigid posture. She didn't know what more they could to her, frozen as she was up on the plinth, until the rocks began to hit her. Unable to bow her head, the sharp edges of the slate and granite cut into her face and neck.

A large rock hit Morgen squarely in the eye and she felt warm blood trickle down her cheek. Her eye throbbed and an ache began in the base of her skull that quickly wrapped around her head like the horns of a ram. Another rock hit her, but didn't do any more damage. The first impact had taken her agony to its highest level. She turned her thoughts inward again as the sharp edges of the rocks continued to inflict their damage. At least the clawing stopped when the rocks were thrown. She guessed the Red Caps at the front of the crowd had retreated so they wouldn't be hit as well.

As the light began to fade with the setting sun, Morgen could barely see out her swollen eyes and her body ached from the constant assault. She watched a Red Cap, taller than most, approach her. Although she could not move, she shrank inwardly from his touch as he reached up and dragged her from her seat. Morgen plummeted to the ground, unable to straighten her legs. She had been frozen in the same position for so long, they wouldn't extend to absorb the impact from the ground. The air left her lungs and she gasped as the Red Cap pulled her to her feet and dragged her through the crowd. As she stumbled behind him, the blood began to flow through her joints again and her movements became more fluid. A Red Cap, possibly one of the three who had kidnapped her, came up beside them.

"Where are you taking her?"

"To the prison."

"Why not just kill her now?"

Morgen gasped at the cold words and then stumbled over a rock in the road to cover her mistake. She was determined they not

153

know she could speak their language. When the Red Caps glared at her she worried they had discovered her secret. She gave a silent thank you when they continued their conversation after a long pause. Her heart pounded in her ears as they continued to argue over her fate. She needed to find a way to escape and she needed to do it before they arrived at the imposing building on the hill. Once she was within those walls, the only way she would leave was as a corpse. Unable to figure out her escape, Morgen slowed her pace as the path continued up a steep hill. She needed to keep her wits about her and find more time to think as the two Red Caps continued their conversation.

"They don't care about her."

"Why not?"

"She isn't married to the dirty cur yet."

The Red Cap snarled at his companion. "What?"

"They have not said their vows."

"But that means—"

"She has no worth to us."

"The ugly wench will not bring us what we want."

The tall Red Cap let out a roar and whirled around to hit Morgen. She took a step back and found she was not restrained. Without another thought, she fluttered her wings. Ignoring the agony searing through her from the torn wing, she rose into the air and labored away from the Red Caps. Tears burned in her eyes as she rose higher. The creatures below her snarled and growled as they brought out their lassos. Morgen gasped for air as she continued to rise higher into the sky and away from their grasping hands and dangerous ropes.

Her wing caused shockwaves of pain. She gritted her teeth against the agony caused with every movement and managed to fly to a treetop. As she clung to the cold trunk, the rough bark bit into her fingers and knifed under her fingernails. She gasped against the constraints of her corset as she tried to catch her breath. Both Red Caps circled below her and continually threw their lassos toward her. The fatal loops came closer and closer. Morgen looked up. There was nowhere higher she could go. She needed to escape. Angered at the failure of the lassos, one of the Red Caps tried to climb the tree. Filled with fear, she took a deep breath and pushed away from the tree. She dipped low in the air as her wings beat a rapid rhythm. She reached for the next tree and drew in a staccato breath as her fingers wrapped around a branch.

Weak, almost paralyzed by pain, she managed to fly from tree to tree until she was several yards ahead of them. Dark clouds hung ominously low as she continued to move away from the city square. Rain began to fall, which provided her with better camouflage, but made the trees slick. The Red Caps crashed through the underbrush behind her and she knew she could not slow her pace. Her hair streamed in her face and her cloak weighed her down as it became sodden. She pulled it off and stuffed it into the union of several branches and the tree trunk. She pulled off the shreds of her petticoats and hid them, too. Lighter, she managed to leapfrog past several more trees.

Pain made her pause in a tree as she fought to dispel a woozy dizziness that suddenly engulfed her. While she drew in a deep breath, her grip slipped on the rain-slicked trunk and she slid down several feet. The bark shredded her palms and sent searing pain through her hands as she worked to keep from crashing to the forest floor. She battled her way back to the top of the tree and pressed her forehead against the tree as she tried to ignore the pain in her ribs. Each breath brought a wave of nausea as she expanded her lungs. Clenching her teeth in determination, she climbed up several branches and flew to the next tree.

Her tears mixed with the rain and together they washed away the blood she left on the bark as she gripped a branch. She curled into a ball and allowed a few moments of self-pity before shaking herself. "No time for that." She forced herself to find her next target tree and threw herself toward it with all the energy she could muster. A branch caught her in the middle and pressed against her cracked ribs. She couldn't stop a cry from cutting through the air. The crashing in the underbrush below her paused and she could hear the Red Caps calling out to her. She climbed up as far as she could and leapt toward the next tree. Over and over she repeated the same routine as she leapt to the next tree, climbed up to regain the height she lost, and then paused to catch her breath and tamp down her dizziness and nausea.

"I can't go on." Her whisper was carried away on the wind. Morgen pressed her forehead against the trunk of the tree she clung to and fell back to pinging Stephen. "Help me. I do not think I will make it to the border. They are just behind me." She squeezed her eyes shut and drew in a breath before pulling her shredded strength around her. As she peered around the trunk to decide on her next target, Stephen's face flashed before her. She gasped as her heartrate accelerated at his ping.

"Stephen?"

"Morgen." The relief in his voice caused more tears to fall. "Come to me."

"Is it really you?"

"Yes."

"This could be a trick. How do I know you are not trying to draw me out?"

"You know me. Trust me."

Tears clouded her vision as she gripped the tree. "I do not know what to trust. Who to trust."

"You can trust me."

She tried to blink her tears away and saw a dark form reach for her. "No!"

"Morgen, it is I."

She swiped at the tears and looked again. Stephen's face and form came into focus. "Am I imagining you?"

"Sire, we must depart."

He looked away and nodded. "Come, Morgen. We must get back to Carlow. The Caps will be upon us."

"I cannot be sure it is you. You could be a Red Cap trick."

"Take my hand. You will know it is me."

"If it is not you, I will be a prisoner once again."

"If we are here much longer, all will be prisoners."

She thought about this for a moment. "Come one step closer. No more."

"Morgen." He came closer, but her eyes still would not focus properly.

"Tell me something only Prince Stephen would know."

"You are my intended."

She scoffed. "That is known to many."

"That night on the bridge, I promised my love. You still have it."

His words pierced her heart and she allowed a momentary flicker of hope to flare within her. "Stephen?"

"Come."

Morgen reached for the hand held out to her and knew it belonged to Stephen. "I cannot fly well."

"I know. I will help you."

Heavy footfalls sounded below them. She gasped. "The Red Caps."

"Yes, they are below." His voice was tight. "Come with me." Stephen clasped her hand and pulled her tightly to his side. His arm wrapped around her waist as they flew through the treetops. Morgen flew the best she could, knowing Stephen would support her and help her. Several Carlowian knights flanked the couple as they moved slowly through the trees toward the border. Morgen recognized one from the morning when she was taken. He was Sir

Thomas, if she recalled correctly, and a particular friend of Lady Fern.

As the sounds of the Red Caps thrashing through the forest began to fade, Morgen allowed herself to relax just a little. She sighed in relief and Stephen strengthened his hold around her. She gasped as he compressed her ribs and he looked at her in concern.

"It is just a bit further."

She nodded and tried to ignore her pain. It was becoming difficult to maintain level flight. She could not coordinate her wings and was unable to judge distances as her vision began to fail.

Thomas came up beside her. "If you please, Princess." He slipped his arm around the middle of her back and helped support her.

"The border is just ahead."

The group slowed to a hover and then descended to the ground. Morgen allowed her wings to droop as she leaned against Stephen's side. Her head lolled to the side and Stephen pressed it against his shoulder. She gripped his free hand and worked to stay conscious.

"This will be difficult."

She nodded. "Yes, I remember."

Three knights pointed their wands at the border. It shimmered and then opened in a jagged vee. Stephen guided Morgen through and a wave of pain washed through her. She couldn't hold back a cry of pain as she stumbled into the no-man's-land. Stephen caught her before she crumpled to the ground. He swept her up in his arms and brought her across the border into Carlow. Morgen looked at the trees and peaceful lake and smiled. "I am home." She allowed herself to fall into the dark abyss that had beckoned for so long.

Chapter Seven

Stephen held Morgen's limp form in his arms as the remaining knights emerged through the border. Once all were present, he pinged Lord O'Conor at the Border Council to close and harden the border against a likely retaliatory breach by the Red Caps.

"We must get her to the palace."

Sir Thomas nodded. "I will notify Lady Fern and the other Gildeds. They will heal her."

Stephen brought Morgen tightly to his chest and the group rose into the air. In the cool evening air, she snuggled closer to him and sighed. Stephen's heart reached out for her as he rushed toward the palace. She had endured so much, judging from the blood and swelling on her face and arms. Her gown was shredded, her cloak gone, and her wing was torn. He couldn't imagine the fortitude it had taken to escape the Caps and fly with her wing in that condition. One of her eyes was so swollen, it was a mere slit. No wonder she had not known him.

"Stephen?"

He looked down at her. "Yes?"

"Thank you."

He smiled as she fell away into slumber again. "I will always come for you." He knew she heard his promise, even though she was unconscious. It was the soft smile that curved her lips that gave him hope.

"Sire, The Gildeds await us."

He looked at Sir Thomas and nodded.

"They have opened the window off the north terrace and removed the spell to allow entry. Go directly through there to the suite. A settee has been arranged for her healing. I requested the assistance of four Gildeds." Sir Thomas paused. "Do you think that will be enough?"

Stephen looked down at Morgen's swollen face. "Likely, she could not endure more healing than four. It will cause quite a bit of pain."

Thomas bowed. "Is there anything else I can do for you, m'lord?"

"No." He paused. "Yes. Arrange for guards at all the windows and doors." He looked at the knights surrounding them. He knew

162

them all well, yet did not know where the danger within the palace lay. "Tell no one of Morgen's condition or whereabouts. Instruct them all."

He watched Thomas confer with Sir Philip, the senior knight, and rapidly the remaining knights nodded. They had received the ping. As he let out a breath of relief, Morgen moaned. He quickened his pace. "We shall be with The Gildeds very soon, dearest."

Within moments they crossed into the protected air around the palace. He followed the lead knights to the open window. Several Gildeds waved him to a settee. He set Morgen gently in place. Four Gildeds immediately surrounded her as the knights took up their positions at all the portals. Stephen released her hand and stepped away as a dense curtain of gold glitter was conjured to protect the princess' modesty. As he moved away, Morgen became restless and babbled incoherently.

"Please, Your Highness, return to her side."

Stephen knelt beside her shoulder.

"Hold her hand."

He did as requested by the serious Gilded. Morgen's restlessness ceased and the strain in her features softened.

"Do not leave her side."

"I will not."

"Stay at her shoulder. You are not permitted through the golden veil."

"Certainly not." Stephen bristled at the suggestion he would compromise Morgen's virtue.

"We will remove the remnants of her gown. She is hidden by the veil on all sides."

Stephen saw the tattered skirts slide to the floor, the ragged torn edges tinged with dried blood. She was not wearing her cloak and, from the lack of fullness under her skirts, had been divested of her petticoats. His body tightened at the thought of those horrible creatures touching her. What she had endured! The Gildeds murmured to each other but he was able to hear some phrases.

"Several broken ribs."

"Deep gashes."

"Scars will always be visible here."

He clenched his teeth together when Morgen cried out in pain. As her pain worsened, so did her cries. Tears ran down her cheeks.

"She cannot endure so much."

The senior Gilded leaned out from behind the veil and pierced him with her gaze. "She can and she will. Do what you can to calm her. Talk to her. We have much to do."

As The Gilded returned to her obscured position, Stephen leaned closer to Morgen and whispered words of encouragement. She calmed a little, but not enough to suit him.

Finally, a Gilded came and knelt beside him. "I shall heal the wounds on her face, neck, and shoulders. Please continue to calm her." She smiled and touched his arm. A warm sense of peace swirled through him. "You are doing a fine job."

As Stephen leaned close to Morgen's ear and whispered to her,

The Gilded placed her hands across the princess' eyes. When she removed them, Morgen's eyes were no longer swollen and the cut over one was gone. He could see a scar running from under her left eye and across her cheek before disappearing into her hairline. It wasn't obvious, but the thin white line marred her delicate skin.

The Gilded rested with her palms on her thighs and hung her head while drawing in deep breaths. "I could not rid her entirely of the marks."

"I understand." He traced the scar with his thumb.

"She will also bear the marks of the Red Caps on her ankles and along her side. She indicated an area over her right ribs. "Here."

Anger build within him as he listened to The Gilded. Morgen didn't deserve such treatment, even at the hands of the Red Caps.

The Gilded placed her hand on his arm. "The time of reckoning will occur. It cannot be rushed."

"How long until then?"

"I cannot say." He put her hand on his arm again and the welcomed sense of peace filled him once more. "Focus on the present. You have much to accomplish here. Now."

He looked down at Morgen. She deserved his full attention as she transitioned into her role within his kingdom. He had not done well by her so far. As he studied her, she elevated off the settee and turned until she was face down.

"Keep talking to her. You bring her peace." The Gilded moved back to the veil. "We shall attend to the wounds on her back and the back of her legs and ankles."

"All this time you have been working only on one side?"

"Her wounds were extensive."

He nodded as The Gilded disappeared. Bending back down, he continued to encourage Morgen. He tucked her hair behind her ear, frowning at the spots where the hair had obviously been torn from her scalp. Likely, that wouldn't have happened had her hair been in her traditional braids. He closed his eyes to the sharp pain that knifed through him at the thought that his own prejudice against Meath had caused her to change her hairstyle, and ultimately caused her pain.

Finally, she was rotated until she was face up. The soft cloth of a night dress emerged from the golden veil and slipped over her head, followed by a cherry pink wrapper. The golden veil shimmered and disappeared and Morgen was fully visible, floating above the settee and surrounded by the four Gildeds who healed her. Lady Isabelle, the senior Gilded, looked at him without her normal smile. "She is prepared. You may take her to her rooms."

When he lifted her into his arms, Morgen immediately snuggled against his chest, just as she had during their flight to the palace. The movement was endearing and he lost a bit more of his heart to her. Knights fell into step around him as he carried her through the door of The Gildeds' Suite and down the corridor. Once they arrived at her rooms, the knights dispersed to their positions in the sitting room and the bed chamber. Lady Fern accompanied him to the bed and drew down the coverings. He placed Morgen gently upon the soft mattress and covered her up to her chin. When he stepped away, she became restless again and cried out his name.

Immediately, he knelt by the bed and held her hand between his palms. Lady Fern moved a chair close to him. He smiled at her gratefully.

She smiled in return. "I shall stay with you for appearances." She motioned another chair into position on the other side of the bed and settled into it.

Stephen transferred into his own chair, never releasing his hold on Morgen's hand. He pinged Lily. She arrived minutes later, out of breath and eyes wide at the sight of Morgen's sleeping form.

"Speak to no one of the princess' condition. No one can know how she was injured." He waited for her to agree. "You must have hot tea waiting for her when she awakens. I will not require that you maintain a hot meal, but you must keep tea and small sandwiches at the ready."

"Yes, Your Royal Highness."

"Devonshire cream, too. And strawberry jam. Scones." He wanted to provide anything she might desire. "Have the fire in the sitting room lit and keep it blazing. Set a fire in here, too. Princess Morgen deserves a warm room when she desires to leave her bed."

"Yes, sir."

Stephen looked at her pale face and tried to soften his tone. "Do not allow anyone else to brew her tea or make her a plate of food without your presence. You are her guardian."

Lily nodded mutely.

"I shall contact my mother. She can provide all the food from our manor." Lady Fern waited for his nod and then moved to the window. He knew she would ping her mother the request, and that Lady O'Conor would be discreet.

"No one is allowed to enter these rooms. The knights will see to that." Stephen paused and kept his gaze on the little fairy, who had begun to tremble. "Take care what happens to Princess Morgen. What she experiences will be wrought on you as well."

Lily paled further.

"You may go."

She curtseyed to him and quickly left for the sitting room. Once she disappeared through the doorway, Stephen turned his attention back to Morgen and combed her hair from her face with his fingers. "You will be safe." He looked up at Lady Fern. "She will be safe, right?"

She nodded with a smile. "I believe so."

Flashes of evil Red Cap faces and the feeling of their sharp claws slicing into her skin filled Morgen's dreams. She cried out as fear swirled through her and her heartrate quickened.

A soothing voice broke through the terrifying imagery. "Shh. You are safe. Nothing will hurt you."

She clung to the strong, warm hand that held hers and focused on the deep timbre of the voice that reassured her. She didn't want the voice to stop or the hand that held hers to go away. Strength was pouring into her from his touch. Thankfully, the voice continued and she fell away into a dark spiral. Soon peaceful darkness enveloped her.

The darkness was replaced by a warm meadow filled with colorful flowers. The fragrance of the flowers and swaying grasses wafted toward her on gentle currents of air. The tension in her shoulders drained away as she continued to walk in the sunlight. As she continued toward the distant mountains, the air turned cooler and icy fingers gripped her throat. It became difficult to breathe as the fingers squeezed tighter, pressing on her wind pipe and against the arteries and veins at the sides of her neck. Morgen wheezed as she drew in a breath and clawed at the fingers wrapped around her throat. Her feet kicked and she arched back and away.

A familiar face swam into view as she continued to struggle for breath. She knew he belonged in Carlow, but could not place how she knew him. In her memory, however, he was not evil. In fact, she associated him with 'friend' or 'ally'. But now, his mouth was twisted into a snarl and his eyes were hard and dark. He spewed hatred at her with his hand tightly around her throat, drawing her strength away. She tried to pull in a breath but none came. Stars pricked her vision and she began to float through a dark tunnel.

Morgen managed to reach for her wand and withdrew it from the pocket of air at her side. She shot bolts of lightning at the looming figure and sharp arrows at the hand around her throat. Just as she was about to fall over the precipice into eternal darkness, the clamp around her throat loosened. Cool air slid down her throat and filled her lungs. Morgen heard herself take in noisy breaths as pain seared her throat, inside and out. She dropped her wand and put her hands to her neck as the pain intensified. Breathing was necessary, but caused so much agony.

"It is okay now, Morgen. I am here. You are safe again."

She tried to answer Stephen, but couldn't make anything but a raspy sound. Slowly, she awakened from whatever level of consciousness she was currently in and looked into the eyes of her prince. His expression was filled with alarm and concern. She tried again to speak, but was unable.

"Rest." He laid his hand on her forehead in a tender gesture. "You will regain your voice soon."

She nodded and gripped his hand tighter before closing her eyes. "Do not leave me."

"I will stay with you however long you need me."

Her anxiety lessened at his words and she relaxed into the peaceful darkness that surrounded her. Sleep was welcome as long as this wonderful feeling of safety remained.

Stephen watched as Morgen's features softened and some of the anxiety left her face. He held her hand as he looked to Ladies Fern and Isabella. The senior Gilded had been summoned when the most recent attack first began. Both Gildeds leaned over Morgen and he could see them concentrate.

"Will he return?"

Lady Isabella shook her head. "I do not detect anyone within her subconscious. She is safe." She looked at Stephen. "For now."

His scalp crinkled with adrenaline as he realized the meaning behind her words. Morgen was still in danger from her attacker. It had been a man. Lady Isabella confirmed that fact. That he had tried to kill Morgen by strangulation was backed by the purple bruises that emerged on her throat. The difficulty came in trying to determine who her attacker was. Any fairy with the requisite skills and experience could enter the subconscious plane and assault her.

He sat up quickly. "Lady Isabella, can someone enter the alternate plane from outside our kingdom?"

"No. It cannot be done across borders, just like a ping cannot be sent from one kingdom to the next."

He watched Lady Fern lay her hands on Morgen's neck and close her eyes. Her breathing quickened and she swayed from side to side as the bruises began to fade. The Gilded slumped onto the edge of the bed and propped herself up on her arms.

Stephen looked at her in concern. "Are you well? Should I call someone?"

Lady Isabella laid her hand on his arm. "Healing is a very exhausting experience. Lady Fern will recover in a moment. As she gains experience, she will be able to monitor her energy expenditure so she is not so completely affected."

As the young Gilded took time to regain her energy, Stephen sat in his chair and ran through a mental list of suspects. He could not decide on a single person who would want to hurt his intended.

"Lady Fern, are you recovered?"

"I believe so, thank you." She stood and returned to her chair on the other side of the room.

"Lady Isabella, please stay for a moment."

She nodded in acquiescence.

"May I run my thoughts by the both of you?"

"Of course."

He pinged Sir Thomas and Sir Philip, the elder knight. "I would like you both to be a part of a discussion I am having with The Gildeds."

The two knights came into the room and stood at attention by the door. Stephen informed them of the attack and calmed them as they passionately swore to mete punishment on the one responsible.

"There will be plenty of time for that. What is imperative now is identifying who is responsible."

Everyone in the tight group agreed.

"Lady Isabella assured me the attack must have come from within Carlow."

The knights looked at each other and back to Stephen. "Do you know who?"

"No."

Thomas looked at Lady Fern and back to Stephen. "Other than her kidnapping, have there been any other incidents against Princess Morgen?"

"Why do you discount the Red Caps?"

"They do not have the ability to enter the subconscious plane."

"We did not think they could breach our border."

"True."

Lady Fern stepped forward. "Slicing open the border came from collusion between the Red Caps and the gnomes."

Everyone looked at her.

"Remember?" She looked each in the eye. "Just before the Battle of Revlin I saw them together in the forest. The Red Caps needed the gnomes' expertise and magic to accomplish such a feat." She looked at Sir Philip. "Could the gnomes have helped the Red Caps enter the subconscious plane?"

"Unlikely. The gnomes are scrambling to repair diplomatic ties with Carlow. They highly underestimated the violence of the Red Caps and have disassociated from them."

She frowned at the carpet under her feet. "If you're certain about that, then it means someone from Carlow is responsible for trying to kill their future queen."

Pain sliced through his heart at her words. It was time to confess his poor behavior toward Morgen. "It may be possible to narrow our search a little more."

"How?"

He told them of the neglect Morgen had endured when she first arrived at the palace.

"She is certainly a self-sufficient woman."

He nodded to Sir Philip and looked at his audience. "It was very impressive, and something that should not have occurred. Ignoring my own negligence, there was a severe dereliction of duty by the royal household."

The four agreed.

Sir Philip spoke first. "If these events are related, who could be responsible for both? Who could cause the neglect as well as orchestrate the kidnapping?"

"Who from Carlow would partner with the Red Caps?" Sir Thomas' voice was harsh.

Stephen appreciated his emotional outburst. "Let us share our ideas."

For the next several minutes, they brought forth various names and rejected each with a valid argument. None appeared to have the opportunity to accomplish both offenses against the princess.

Sir Thomas cleared his throat and shifted his weight. "This is rather oblique, but what about the Lord Chamberlain?"

Stephen stared at him in silence. "He is one of my father's most trusted advisors."

"Yes, but he does have the access."

Stephen shook his head. "It cannot be him. If it were—"

"If it were, the king could be in danger as well." Sir Philip put his fists on his hips. "That is cause to investigate this further. I shall send more knights to protect His Majesty."

"We must be careful. If it is he, we do not want to let him know what we suspect."

Sir Philip nodded and stepped away to ping more knights. He returned quickly. "It is done. They shall be discreet and will link the increased security to the kidnapping. It is a valid reason and will not be questioned."

Stephen turned to Sir Thomas. "Convince me again that the

Lord Chamberlain should be one of our suspects."

"Whoever was responsible had access to the servants and enough power to change the orders for her staffing and her care. That same person possibly had enough ability to contact the Red Caps, establish a relationship of trust, and plan the kidnapping."

The argument was convincing. He looked at Sir Philip. "But, the Lord Chamberlain?"

"It was the Lord Chamberlain. That is who I saw."

Stephen whipped around at the sound of Morgen's quiet and rough voice. He leaned down close to her ear. "When did you see him?"

She was silent for so long he thought she had not heard him. "When he tried to strangle me." Her eyes fluttered and her body relaxed. She was unconscious again.

Stephen looked at the knights in disbelief. "What do we do now?"

"We behave under the assumption that the Lord Chamberlain is behind the attacks." Sir Philip's mouth was a grim line. "Both of them."

Stephen stood, but continued to hold Morgen's hand. "Let us find him now."

"No, Your Highness. That would not be wise." Sir Philip stepped forward. "We do not have the evidence we need."

Sir Thomas stepped forward the stand beside his mentor. "We must set a trap."

Stephen looked at the two knights, united in their belief this was the best course of action. "Are you certain the king is protected?"

They nodded. "Additional knights are in place. If you please, we did caution them to surveille against attacks on the subconscious plane."

Stephen nodded. "It was necessary to show our hand in this case. Keep me updated if there are any changes."

The two knights left the room. Before Sir Thomas disappeared through the door, he looked back. "Lady Fern—"

"Princess Morgen will be protected by The Gildeds for as long as necessary." She managed a small smile. "We will not leave her alone."

"When will you sleep?"

"When it is done."

Stephen looked from Lady Fern to Sir Thomas and admired the connection between them. He knew they were romantically involved and hoped to have the same bond with Morgen someday. He looked down at his hand linked with hers. Hopefully, that day would come soon.

Chapter Eight

Morgen gripped the warmth that surrounded her hand and pulled herself from the peaceful embrace of slumber. Her body ached and her throat had a raw edge, though nothing was painful enough to distress her. She stretched a little under the weight of the blankets and opened her eyes. The comforting depths of Stephen's eyes looked back at her. He smiled. Her body filled with more warmth and she returned the smile.

"Hi."

His smile widened. "Hello."

Morgen closed her eyes and snuggled deeper into the bed. "What time is it?"

"It is eleven o'clock."

She looked at him and then to the window. The drapes were closed and she couldn't see outside. "In the morning?"

His laughter caressed her and he squeezed her hand. "It is almost time for lunch."

"What did I miss?" Her anxiety spiraled upward as his expression transitioned from warm and smiling to serious. "What is it?"

"Someone tried to injure you by using the subconscious plane."

The feel of a cold hand squeezing her throat caused her to gasp. "I remember." She put her hand to her throat to protect herself from another attack. "Is that allowed here?"

"Never." His eyes blazed. "It is cowardly and considered a personal assault."

She sandwiched his hand between hers and shifted to face him more fully. "We will find who did this."

He leaned closer. "We know who is responsible."

Morgen's eyes widened. "Who?"

"I will tell you all the details in a few minutes. First, we need to make sure we are secure before we speak."

She drew in a sharp breath. "Then it is someone close." She looked about the room. "Am I safe here?"

"You are with me."

Morgen pushed back her covers. "I need to dress. I cannot be caught in a battle while wearing my nightdress."

Stephen stood quickly ad turned his back to her. "I shall leave you in the presence of Lady Fern. Shall I send in your maid?"

She smiled at his gallantry and quickly donned her wrap. "I have a maid?"

"Lily is at your disposal."

"How wonderful. Thank you, Stephen."

His head began to turn toward her, but he stopped and returned to face the wall. "You are welcome."

Morgen watched him leave the room, then looked at Lady Fern and smiled. The Gilded pushed open the curtains and her wings sparkled in a shaft of sunlight. Morgen smiled as she looked at the view of the garden.

The Gilded stepped into her line of vision. "He has been here the entire time."

She looked at The Gilded and smiled. "Has he?"

"He is very fond of you."

Morgen's cheeks warmed as she looked back out the window. There was no response that came to mind. She did not dare disagree with Lady Fern, yet the fact that her intended was so protective showed a high level of caring and emotion. That fact left her glowing.

"You appear happy."

She looked at Lady Fern. "It is strange, after what happened to me, but it appears all of this has brought me closer to Prince Stephen. It is unexpected.

"It is a wonderful result. I wonder what the person who is behind all of this would think if he knew."

"It will likely make him very angry." Morgen pressed her lips together as she considered the danger that surrounded her. "I must be cautious."

Lily entered the room. "Good morning, Princess Morgen."

"Lily! I am so pleased you are here."

The slight fairy blushed as she busied herself at the armoire. "Do you have a gown in mind for today, or shall I choose one for you?"

Morgen selected a gown that gave her confidence whenever she wore it. With confidence comes power and she needed both to endure what likely lay ahead. Lily helped her into her undergarments and her one remaining petticoat. Once the gown slipped over her shoulders, Lily deftly closed the seam of the bodice. As Morgen sat before her mirror, Lily curled and twirled her hair into a creative design that seemed to meld the braids she preferred with the fall of curls that was fashionable in Carlow.

Morgen smiled at the slight fairy. "You have learned so much since I last saw you."

Lily blushed as she patted Morgen's hair into place. "You look lovely. Prince Stephen is waiting in the sitting room."

Morgen grinned at her through the mirror and stood. After a twirl in the full-length mirror next to the armoire, she squeezed Lily's arm in thanks and went to the outer room. She expected to see Stephen standing alone as he waited for her to dress. Instead he was seated at a table, surrounded by knights.

"Please join us." Stephen indicated a chair at his side. "These knights are to be trusted."

Sir Philip stepped forward. "This room has been placed in isolation. We can speak freely."

Morgen nodded and slipped into the seat next to the prince as he continued to speak. "I will first ensure everyone here has the same information." He quickly stated the facts of the kidnapping and the attack on Morgen's subconscious plane.

Every word heightened her anxiety and she sat on her hands to stop their trembling. Stephen reached over and rubbed small circles on her back. His touch soothed her and Morgen slowed her breathing. As she released her hands from their prison, she smiled at him gratefully.

"We believe the same person masterminded both attacks." He paused and reached for her hand. Morgen welcomed the warmth of his touch. The intensity of his gaze worried her.

"Do you know who?"

He nodded. "The Lord Chamberlain."

Morgen gasped and her fingers involuntarily gripped his hand. "No."

Stephen nodded.

"The king?"

"My father is protected. It is you we must keep safe." He slid from his seat to kneel beside her. "I will not allow him to hurt you again. You must not allow it, yourself. To that end, you must learn to protect yourself."

Her scalp crawled at his words. "Do I join the knights on the training field?"

Her attempt at humor fell flat. He shook his head without even a hint of a smile. "You will train with The Gildeds. They will instruct you in ways to defend yourself against another attack on the subconscious plane."

"I imagine that will take more time than I have available."

He nodded. "It would to become truly proficient. In this case, however, you need only to gain enough skill to fend him off."

"I will do my best."

"Lady Fern will take you into the Gildeds' Suite for your lessons. Their rooms are always secure."

The Gilded materialized at her elbow. "Princess Morgen, we are ready for you."

"Now?"

Fern nodded.

"Morgen?"

She turned to face Stephen and yearned to smooth the lines of concern from around his eyes and mouth.

"With your approval, these knights and I will remain in your rooms to discuss our strategy."

"Of course." Morgen ignored her desire to embrace him to bring forth a smile, and turned away. She followed Lady Fern as they moved quickly from the sitting room to the Gildeds' Suite. Once inside, she marveled at the beautiful furnishings and exquisite gilding throughout.

"You have been here before."

"When?"

Lady Fern smiled. "When we healed you. There is the settee where you lay."

She turned to look around the room. "Nothing is familiar."

"You were unconscious for most of it."

"Oh, dear."

"Do not fret. Your modesty was maintained."

"I was not concerned about that."

"What does concern you?"

Morgen smiled and looked at the rose-patterned carpet under her feet. "Did I say anything untoward in my—" she hesitated— "altered state?"

"No. You were a perfect lady."

"Thank you. I have heard stories where fairies have said things completely out of context. I would be so embarrassed if I said something silly, causing someone I cared about to think less of me."

Several Gildeds approached and introduced themselves. Morgen curtseyed to them and followed them to a comfortable chair placed at a parquetry table. Several Gildeds sat in the other chairs and others stood around her.

Lady Isabella sat to her right and nodded to her. "With your permission, I shall enter your subconscious plane."

Another Gilded leaned forward. "We are not above the laws of our kingdom and cannot enter the plane without permission."

A flash of adrenaline coursed through her. "Then how did he do it?"

"You are susceptible." Lady Isabella reached over and covered Morgen's hand with her own.

"How is it you know how to enter the plane?"

She smiled. "I am the senior Gilded."

Lady Fern, seated on her left, pinged Morgen. "The senior Gilded does not need permission from anyone."

"Not even the king?"

Lady Fern grinned at her pinged response. "They behave as equals, although the senior Gilded is considered higher than he."

"Higher than the king?"

Lady Fern nodded. Morgen looked from her to Lady Isabella and back to Lady Fern, who continued her ping. "She works in partnership with His Majesty."

Morgen stared at her for a full minute before she pulled herself together and turned to face the senior Gilded, knowing she was aware of her pinged conversation with Lady Fern. "Forgive me. I should have known."

Lady Isabella smiled. "Do not berate yourself. You are not expected to know all the traditions and hierarchies of our kingdom this soon after your arrival."

"There are certain basic facts that support a kingdom. One is the king's authority. The second, at least here in Carlow, is your position above him. That is a piece of knowledge I should have had prior to my arrival." She managed a small smile at the effervescent Gilded. "My kingdom and my monarch did me a large disservice by withholding information about Carlow."

Lady Isabella covered her hand with her smooth and warm palm. "We understand your removal from Meath was highly unexpected on your part. Do not worry yourself with the unknown. In time, it will become known to you."

Morgen smiled as peace flowed through her with the touch. "I believe I require lessons on your kingdom and history."

Lady Fern smirked. "Prince Stephen will likely be your best teacher. You should discuss this with him at your next encounter."

The heat of a blush crept up Morgen's throat and face.

"Speaking of lessons, it is time we begin instructing you in defense." As Lady Isabella spoke, Fern rose and another Gilded took her place. "This is Her Exalted Highness Lady Emma."

Morgen nodded and smiled to The Gilded dressed in a gown of soft tangerine orange at the waist that faded to a beautiful golden orange at the hems of her skirts and sleeves. The neckline was accented with streaks of dark red. Swirls of gilded thread sparkled throughout her gown. The faint scent of citrus perfumed the air.

Lady Emma explained how she would enter Morgen's subconscious plane and the steps she should take to eject her. She would gradually increase the power of her assault until Morgen was strong and skilled enough to fight off someone of the same skill level as the Lord Chamberlain.

"I am ready."

Lady Emma closed her eyes and Morgen felt her presence within her mind. She had entered her subconscious plane. Her heart raced and her throat began to close as panic gripped her. Breathing became difficult. She gripped her skirts in tight fists.

"I cannot. I cannot."

The Gilded immediately vacated the plane. Morgen gasped and drew in deep breaths of air.

"Yes." Lady Emma's voice was crisp and factual. "We have much work to do."

Morgen nodded and kept her eyes closed. The experience was unsettling and brought terrible memories to the surface. She longed for Stephen's presence and the feel of his hands holding hers. Instead, the river of peace came at the hands of Lady Emma. It flowed through her and filled her with light and optimism.

"Now, let us discuss strategies to prevent someone from entering the plane, as well as what to do if they get there."

Morgen nodded and gazed into the fairy's warm brown eyes. They spent several hours deliberating possible techniques and practicing them on the subconscious plane. By the time Morgen returned to her rooms with Lady Fern, she was wilted with fatigue and her head ached.

"I will tend to your needs once we are safely within your rooms."

She nodded to the young Gilded.

"I shall have Lily order your dinner. It has been a long time since you shared luncheon with Lady Emma during your training."

Morgen stifled a yawn as she agreed. Lady Fern grinned. "Perhaps we should skip the meal. You look ready for bed."

"Do you think he will trespass upon me tonight?"

The Gilded's smile faded. "I hope not, but we expect it to be soon."

"You will be with me in my chamber while I sleep?"

"Yes, as will Lady Emma. The knights will guard your windows and doors."

Morgen nodded. "It will happen tonight." She looked about her sitting room and spied Lily coming from the bedroom. "I must have strong tea."

Lily curtseyed.

"And dinner."

She curtseyed again.

"Follow Prince Stephen's instructions regarding the preparation of her tea and meals."

Lily nodded and dipped into another curtsey at Lady Fern's instructions. "I have brought what I need to prepare her tea here." She walked to an arrangement of packets of tea leaves and a hand-painted tea pot. "I purchased the tea myself this afternoon." She cast her gaze to the floor. "I did not want to risk any of the tea already purchased for the palace."

"That is very sound thinking." Lady Fern smiled at her. "Well done."

The little servant beamed. "I shall pour tea for myself first and taste it before Princess Morgen has any." She paused and looked from Morgen to Fern. "What should I do to keep her meal safe?"

"The meal will appear here directly from my mother's kitchen.

As a precaution, wash the plate and utensils in hot, soapy water before you fill the plate. Make an identical plate for yourself from the same serving dishes and taste each item before you serve the princess. A Gilded shall be with you to ensure your safety."

Lily nodded as fear flitted in her eyes. Lady Fern crossed the floor and placed her hand on her shoulder. "Do not worry. You are under the protection of The Gildeds, as is Princess Morgen. We will keep you safe."

Morgen smiled at the worship she saw in Lily's eyes. Lady Fern was a warm and friendly fairy who truly cared for those around her. While she and Lily looked to be the same age, there was a significant difference in their mannerisms and temperament.

"Now, stay here in the sitting room while I ping my mother for Princess Morgen's meal. I shall manage the tea."

Lily nodded and curtseyed as she crossed the room to the table by the window to await the meal. Morgen looked at Lady Fern and pressed her lips together. "I am so afraid."

"So am I." She grimaced. "I probably should not have admitted that." She clasped Morgen's hands and gripped them tightly. Morgen hoped for the warm comfort of security and hope to flow through her, but it did not appear.

"Sorry. I have not learned how to share calm and peace."

She shook her head at Lady Fern's apology. "I must find the strength within myself. I cannot rely on you or anyone else to bring me happiness or refuge from darkness."

"You are lucky to learn that lesson. Now you are able to provide those things to others."

Morgen smiled as Lady Fern deftly fixed a pot of tea. They walked together into the bedroom. "I wish I could sleep in armor or a doublet. I do not relish the idea of fighting while in my nightgown."

"It is your dream." Lady Fern poured a steaming cup of tea and handed it to her. "You may wear what you wish."

"Truly?"

She nodded.

"Then I choose breeches and a leather doublet. And a dirk." Morgen laughed softly. "And a team of Gildeds behind me."

"We will be there, but you won't have any need for us. You did so well during your lessons that you can manage your subconscious plane well enough on your own."

"I had the lessons, but I do not know if I will remember what to do. What if he attacks me and my mind goes blank?"

Lady Fern gripped her arm. "It won't. Do not doubt yourself. With doubt comes weakness."

Morgen drew in a deep breath and tried to tamp down her reservations. She managed to decrease them, but a small thorn of uncertainty remained.

"Believe in yourself, in your strength. That is your power."

She looked at The Gilded and sighed. "How do I rid myself of all my doubts? There is a small voice in my head that continually questions my resolve."

"You must believe in yourself." Lady Fern stared deeply into

Morgen's eyes. "Do not allow that voice to speak." Her gaze was intense and bored into her. "At the very least, do not listen to it. Pretend it is a sprite speaking in that really high-pitched voice they have. You know how irritating it is to listen to them."

Morgen grinned and turned to the window. The shoulder of a knight could be seen through the crystalline glass. Comforted by the sight of one of her protectors, she drew the curtains and turned back toward Lady Fern. "I suppose it is time."

Lily arrived with a tray covered with dishes. Morgen managed a few bites before she pushed the tray away. "I am sorry." She smiled to Lily before she placed her napkin on the tray. "I am too nervous to eat."

"That is understandable." Lady Fern waved her hand over the tray and it disappeared. "Why don't you take some tea and then Lily will prepare you for bed."

Morgen nodded and sipped the black tea that was lightly spiced with cinnamon and sugar. "This is wonderful. What is it called?"

"It is my own recipe." Lily clasped her hands before her and flushed prettily. "I'm glad you enjoy it."

"I do. I hope to enjoy it often."

Lily cast her gaze to the floor for a moment and suddenly ran to Morgen's side. "Please stay safe." Her eyes filled with tears. "You are very special." Her blush deepened. "Was that too personal? I have been admonished for taking too many liberties with those above my station."

"It was not too personal." She pulled Lily into an embrace.

"You are very special, too. Never forget that."

Lily's smile showed her pleasure even as she avoided Morgen's searching eyes. Lady Fern slipped out of the room and closed the door as Lily moved behind Morgen and applied her wand to the back seam of Morgen's gown. Once it was open, Morgen raised her arms and her day frock and petticoats floated away. Once dressed in her nightgown and wrapper, Morgen sat at the dressing table and Lily pulled out her hair pins. She closed her eyes as Lily brushed through her tresses and gently wove her hair into two fat braids. Lady Emma came into the room as she slipped under the covers and rested her head on the freshly plumped pillows.

"How are you feeling?"

Morgen smiled as she snuggled under her bedding.

"Do not be afraid. Lady Fern and I will be by your side all night."

Lady Fern came into the room and took a seat in the chair she had occupied all day.

Morgen smiled to her and turned her attention back to Lady Emma. "And the knights will remain at the portals?"

The Gilded nodded in confirmation. "You are well-protected."

Morgen rested her arms at her sides above the covers and settled into the wonderfully comfortable mattress. "I am ready."

Despite her best efforts, it took Morgen almost a half-hour to fall asleep. She began to dream of a peaceful walk through a beautiful meadow. She was filled with expectation as she searched for Stephen, the only one she wanted to meet in this beautiful spot.

Her skirts swished through the tall grasses and the sunlight warmed her shoulders. The feel of her hair trailing down her back was unexpected. She reached back and was surprised to find it was not in the braids Lily had so deftly woven, but in the Carlowian fall of curls. Funny.

A figure appeared at the far end of the meadow. Morgen smiled and quickened her pace as she anticipated meeting with Stephen. Low-lying plants tugged at her petticoats as she stepped through the grass. Colorful flowers waved on slender stems in the light breeze. She suppressed the urge to collect a bouquet and continued toward the figure that remained shrouded in the shadows of the trees that edged the field.

"Stephen!" Her voice resonated through the air.

The figure lifted a hand in greeting. As she quickened her pace the sunlight brightened before her, making it difficult to see. As the sound of Stephen's footfalls thudded dully in the warm soil, Morgen felt her throat begin to close. The vise-like grip of a strong hand began to squeeze her throat even as she continued to walk alone, with none beside her.

"Stephen!" Her voice was little more than a croak.

A low, masculine voice hissed in her ear. "Just die."

Adrenaline coursed through her as she tried to focus her energies into managing her subconscious plane. With effort, Morgen managed to force the hand from her throat and drew in a long, wheezy breath. "Who are you?" She could not see the figure's features in the harsh sunlight. One thing was certain, it was not Stephen.

"I am the one who will protect the great land of Carlow from being tainted by the blood of Meath."

Morgen's heartbeat pounded in her ears. "Is that your duty?"

"My duty is to ensure the security and comfort of the kingdom and the monarch of Carlow."

The figure grabbed her arm. When he moved, he blocked the bright sunlight. Morgen's eyes adjusted to the light and she gasped to see the features of the Lord Chamberlain. "You!"

"You should not have allowed yourself to be accessed like this." He held his hand out before him and squeezed. The now-familiar tightening occurred around her throat, blocking her air flow. Morgen managed to repel him and took several steps back and to the side as she filled her lungs. Anger distorted the Lord Chamberlain's features as his attack was thwarted. "You are stronger than I expected." He lunged toward her. "It will not be enough."

Morgen twirled away and stared at him with narrowed eyes. "I am more than enough." She blocked him with her mind and forced him back a few feet. He let out a low, guttural snarl and flung energy at her. She managed to deflect it and cast her gaze about for defense. She spied a large boulder and ran to take shelter.

"That granite is no match."

She worked to steady her breathing and conserve her energy. The air became thick and she knew the Lord Chamberlain neared. Stepping out from the protection of the boulder, she flung her own energy toward him. He paused and snarled again. Morgen hurled more energy toward him. Despite the strength she gained from the support of Stephen and The Gildeds, the Lord Chamberlain was stronger. Her energy pushed him back a step, but he managed to take two toward her. The gap between them diminished and soon she could hear his raspy breath and smell the stench of dried sweat and the metallic smell of deep anger.

"I will not deny you have skills, yet you are not enough."

Morgen swallowed her retort and concentrated on conserving her energy. She needed to focus on the siege, not the small victories. She could not lower her guard.

"You will never be enough." The Lord Chamberlain took a step toward her. Morgen did not attempt to stop him. "You are the seed of a coward. Your tainted blood will not mix with the royal House of Mulryan."

"I believe, Lord Chamberlain, that your argument is with your king, not me."

"If you are removed, there will be no argument." He held out his hand again and attempted to choke her.

"Unhand me."

"Such a highhanded tone for a low-born trollop."

"You have no right—"

"I have every right." His grip tightened and his fingernails dug into the tender skin of her upper arm. "You are the one with no rights here."

Morgen pulled her power around her and pushed him away. An

expression of surprise crossed his features as he was moved several feet away. Morgen rubbed her arm where the pain from his grip continued to sear her skin. She narrowed her eyes at him. "Take care, Lord Chamberlain. You tread upon dangerous ground."

He took a step closer and she forced him away again. "You have honed your skills." He forced her power away and began to close the distance between them. Again, she managed to focus her power and push him away. A sneer crossed his face. Morgen was shocked to discover how much he enjoyed their sparring. She worked to ignore the little voice that told her she could not beat this man and concentrated on her newfound abilities to protect herself.

"You will never marry the prince."

"I will."

With each sentence, the Lord Chamberlain took a step toward her. She managed to repeatedly repel him but fatigue began to creep into her shoulders from the effort. An evil glint appeared in his eyes as he appeared to sense her fading power. Morgen dug deep down and tried to find a reservoir of energy to continue her fight.

Chapter Nine

As the Lord Chamberlain pushed against her power and took a few steps toward her, a sense of security and confidence infused Morgen.

"Thank you, Lady Emma." She tried to hide her smile as The Gilded lent her some much-needed support. Morgen tossed her hair over her shoulder and forced her exhaustion down into a deep corner. Determined to see this fight through to the end, whatever that may be, she set her feet more firmly on the packed earth and squared off against her foe. As he came at her in a surge of energy, Morgen tucked her chin into her shoulder to lessen the effects of his attack and prepared herself to take the mental portrait. With a sudden move, she turned to face him and concentrated to capturing his angry features and outstretched arm.

"What have you done?" His face contorted into an even more grotesque expression.

As her last reserve of energy spiraled away, Morgen collapsed to the ground in a heap of skirts and petticoats. The Lord Chamberlain snarled at her and pulled a dirk from his waistband. She could only watch as he raised it over his head and aimed the lethal blade at her heart.

"Stop!"

She turned toward the commanding voice and saw Stephen charge through the grasses. He brandished his sword, as did the knights who surrounded him. Fear flickered in the Lord Chamberlain's face as he glanced at them. In a move that reeked of desperation, he swiped the blade toward her. Morgen flung her arm up to deflect the blow and the sharp edge of the dagger sliced into her forearm. The pain was white-hot and took her breath away. A small cry sounded from her as she kicked out at him and tried to make any sort of impact. He grunted as she made contact on his shin with the hard heel of her leather boot. She continued to attack him from the ground as the warm stickiness of her own blood coursed down her arm. The pounding of the running prince and knights came closer as she continued to kick her feet and punch blindly. With one well-timed kick, she hit him squarely in the knee. He collapsed into a kneel and the dagger dropped from his hand.

Morgen scrambled to her feet and grabbed the dagger. "Stay down." Her voice cracked with emotion as she pointed the tip of the blade at him. "I will use this." She waggled the knife. "Do not doubt me."

The Lord Chamberlain scowled at her and moved to rise.

"I said stay down." She pressed the tip of the blade into his shoulder and it easily sliced through the velvet sleeve of his coat. The blade was sharper than she thought. That was good. She didn't think she could continue to fight him. Taking the mental picture had taken all her strength.

"Morgen, we are here. You may stand down."

Stephen's voice came to her through a mist. She continued to stare down at the Lord Chamberlain. "You are finished. You will not bully me or anyone else. Not again." She pressed the knife blade deeper, until he winced.

"Morgen."

She shook her head at Stephen, but kept her gaze on her enemy. "He cannot be allowed to continue."

Stephen put his hand over hers and gently drew the dagger away from the man's shoulder. "He will not. I will make sure of it."

With her hand curled into a fist, she stared at the Lord Chamberlain and his face morphed into her father's. "You have hurt me long enough. Now it is time for me to press back. You will not make me feel small any longer." Morgen leaned closer to him as Stephen put his hand on her shoulder. He did not attempt to pull her away from the traitor, instead lending her strength and support as she continued to vent her emotions. "You will not make me feel unwanted. I am worthy of consideration. I am valued. I am loved." Stephen began to stroke her back. "I am worthy."

Morgen straightened and looked at her prince and the knights who surrounded him. "I am worthy and expect to be treated as such."

The knights agreed with much murmuring and nodding. She nodded back once and looked at Stephen. "Any questions?"

He grinned. "No, Your Highness."

"Good. Now, can we leave my subconscious and get on with real life?"

His smile widened. "Absolutely."

Morgen sat on the edge of her bed and longed to bury herself in the soft sheets and thick blankets. She wanted to hide until this entire mess was resolved and she was safe again. Yet, confidence and satisfaction coursed through her. It was a strange thing to have such opposite feelings inside. Deliberately, she forced away her fatigue and embraced the inner power that filled her like magic. She had done the most difficult task and had managed to take the picture of the Lord Chamberlain as he attempted to assault her. Not only that, but she had asserted herself and demanded respect. She smiled and hugged herself.

"What has you so happy?"

She grinned at Lady Fern, who had healed the wound on her arm from the Lord Chamberlain's dirk just a moment before.

"Life is wonderful, is it not?"

Lady Fern returned her smile. "It is. Absolutely."

Lady Emma came through the door with a force that startled Morgen. "Princess Morgen, you must dress right away." Lady Emma looked from her to the door and back to her. "Prince Stephen awaits you in the sitting room. He must retrieve your mental portrait."

Morgen nodded and stood in her nightgown, the bloodied gown and petticoats had disappeared once she awakened from her time in the subconscious plane. She shivered in the cold night air as Lily hurried into the bed chamber and deftly fitted her into a serviceable day dress. In a manner of minutes, her hair was pulled back in a simple style and she was prepared for the next steps in this horrible business.

She patted her hair absently and crossed the threshold into the sitting room with Ladies Emma and Fern. The knights continued to guard her windows and doors. Prince Stephen stood facing a window with his hands clasped behind him. He turned as she entered the room and hurried across the floor to her side.

"How is your arm?"

She looked down at it. "Healed."

He nodded to The Gildeds who stood beside her before turning his gaze back to Morgen. "How are you? In general, I mean?"

"I am fine. Thank you for coming to my rescue when the Lord Chamberlain—" She bit her words off, unwilling to be reminded of the attack.

"You did not need any rescuing."

She tried to smile, but could not manage more than a slight curve to her lips. "I was glad for you anyway."

He cupped her elbow and led her to the settee. "It is time to retrieve the evidence you gathered."

Adrenaline coursed through her at the thought of returning to the dark and forbidding place where others had unnatural power over her. Stephen appeared to understand her reticence and stroked the back of her hand with his thumb. It was remarkably soothing.

"You will be safe."

She considered his expression and tilted her head. "If so, then why do you grimace?"

"Did I?"

She nodded.

"I do not look forward to presenting this to my father." He drew in a breath. "He has bestowed the Lord Chamberlain with his complete trust. This betrayal will hurt him deeply."

Morgen nodded and could not think of anything reassuring to say to him. She felt him attempt to enter her subconscious plane. She gripped his hand. "Please wait. I need a few more minutes to gather myself before I open myself to you."

Stephen jerked as if hit and faced her squarely. His brow furrowed and his expression was dark. "I have not yet tried to enter your mind."

"Someone is." Stephen scooted closer to her and held her hands. She closed her eyes and worked to put up the barriers she had learned from The Gildeds earlier that afternoon. She took strength from Stephen's presence and the feel of his hand laced with hers. After repelling the unknown assailant multiple times, she looked up at the prince and frowned. "Whoever it is keeps trying."

"You can beat him. Keep at it."

Morgen leaned closer to him and closed her eyes. Over and over she resisted the attempts until fatigue washed over her. The gentle lilt of Stephen's voice comforted her as he whispered words of encouragement. Drawing in a stabilizing breath, she looked at him. "You must stop him."

Stephen looked deeply into her eyes, wishing he could take her into his arms and hold her close. However, without the marriage ceremony, before these knights and ladies, he could do no more than simply touch his hand to hers. "We have shown our hand. I must go to the king."

She nodded. "Go. You must protect him."

"I must take some knights with me." He stood and gestured to several. "I will not leave you unprotected."

He walked to Sir Philip. "Stay and protect the princess. I will take some of the knights to the king. Ping others you trust to meet me at the throne room. We must alert him before the Lord Chamberlain can protect himself."

As Sir Philip did as he was bid, Stephen returned to Morgen. "I must retrieve the portrait."

She straightened her spine. "I am ready."

He swept her into a fierce hug, protocol be damned. "Where does this strength and mental fortitude grow within you?"

She laughed against his shoulder. "Perhaps I will share that with you one day."

He pulled back from her and looked into her eyes. She mesmerized him with her dark eyes flecked with gold. "You are a most beguiling girl." Her self-conscious giggle endeared her to him even more. "I look forward to our wedding and marriage with great anticipation."

She flushed and looked down, shielding her eyes with thick lashes. "As do I."

As he reached out to stroke her cheek, the sound of someone clearing his throat forced his hand back to his lap. "M'lord, it is time." Reluctantly, he released his hold of Morgen's hand. "Take care. He remains a threat." As she nodded, Stephen looked to the three Gildeds who surrounded his princess. "Watch over her. Please."

They nodded. "You have our word, Your Royal Highness. Naught will happen to Princess Morgen in your absence."

"Thank you, Lady Emma. Lady Isabella." He looked each one directly. "Lady Fern." They nodded and flanked Morgen. Lady Isabella remained standing behind her. He quickly retrieved the portrait and reluctantly left her side. With The Gildeds protecting Morgen, he hurried to the king's side. Servants and courtiers scattered from their path as he and his group of knights ran to the throne room. Stephen was beyond caring about their blatant

203

curiosity. Let their tongues wag and the stories circulate the palace. He must protect his father from the Lord Chamberlain.

"Father!" He strode through the door to the throne room and made his way through the clusters of subjects awaiting their time to petition the king.

The king looked away from the man before him and scowled at his son. "Please approach."

Stephen stood close to his father's right hand and bent down to whisper in his ear. "I must speak to you immediately."

"I am in the middle of an adjudication session."

"This is imperative."

His father regarded him for a moment before nodding his assent. Stephen followed him to the antechamber attached to the throne room. Once the door closed, he whirled to face the king. "There is a threat within the palace."

"Slow down, Stephen. Tell me what you know."

Stephen related the Lord Chamberlain's actions to his father.

"I cannot believe he would do these things. You must be mistaken."

"I have proof."

"The only acceptable evidence is a confession. He is my closest advisor. I will not accuse him of these actions with less."

"I have the evidence you require." The king's face drained of color as he received the mental portrait.

"How can this be?" The king looked at his son. "He looks as though he were choking someone." He paced the floor. "Against whom was this crime committed?"

"Princess Morgen."

Fury blazed in the king's eyes. "She is our guest and under my protection."

Stephen held out his hands in supplication.

"Call him to the throne room."

"I believe, Father, he will ignore my summons. I rescued Princess Morgen from him while on her subconscious plane."

"This was done on her plane?"

Stephen nodded. "He attacked her there at least twice and was attempting to enter it again as I left to find you. The Gildeds have been assisting and protecting her."

"The Lord Chamberlain assaulted our choice for the future queen of Carlow on her subconscious plane?"

He nodded again. "She managed to repel him and take the mental portrait."

"She is strong."

He couldn't keep the smile from his lips. "She is—" He paused—"amazing."

The king paused. "We have called the Lord Chamberlain to the throne room. Stay out of sight until we confront him."

Stephen bowed in agreement and kept the door slightly ajar as his father returned to his ornate chair. The Lord Chamberlain arrived soon after, his eyes furtive as he scanned the room. Stephen smiled slightly at the relief evident on the man's face as he approached the king. The knights had effectively melted into the crowd and there was no sign of disapproval from any of those present. The man had no idea what awaited him.

"Lord Chamberlain." The king's voice boomed through the room. Subjects and courtiers quieted their conversations and turned to watch the powerful man approach their monarch. Stephen knew they smelled blood in the water. He didn't know how, but they always knew.

The king continued, using a friendly and conversational tone. "We hear you are dissatisfied with our choice of bride for the royal prince."

The Lord Chamberlain drew himself up to his fullest height. "Meathians are not worthy."

"Not worthy?"

Stephen knew his father was baiting the man, allowing him to verbally dig himself into a deep hole.

"No. They are a vile race and a filthy kingdom."

"And?"

"Their dirty blood should not be mixed with that of Your Majesty's."

The king remained silent.

"Our future king or queen should not be tainted by the cowardly blood of the Meathians. His Royal Highness deserves—We deserve—a princess royal who is beautiful and well-mannered. Someone who will be a credit to our kingdom."

Stephen tightened his grip on the door handle, but resisted rushing out to defend Morgen. His father would handle the Lord

Chamberlain very well.

"Princess Fruhlingsmorgen from Meath does not fill those requirements?"

"Absolutely not." The Lord Chamberlain took a step closer to the king, which allowed Stephen a better view of the man from his place behind the door. "She is a coarse and crude girl without manners or beauty. Sire, may I be honest?"

The king nodded slowly to give his assent, which appeared to buoy the Lord Chamberlain's courage to speak.

"She will not bring honor to the House of Mulryan. Her children will be cowardly and weak. She must be returned whence she came and another bride, a better bride, chosen for His Royal Highness."

"If we are not mistaken, you are charging us with making an incorrect choice for Prince Stephen."

"No, Sire. No." The Lord Chamberlain waved his hands before him and stepped closer. "The information provided to Your Majesty was likely faulty and filled with inaccuracies."

The king rose from his throne in a slow and deliberate manner. "We hear you have insulted Her Royal Highness by entering her subconscious plane."

A gasp arose from the onlookers.

"Y-Y-Your Majesty?"

"You attacked the royal princess on her subconscious plane."

"I-I was protecting Carlow."

"And this gives you the liberty to attack the princess?"

"It was necessary."

"Enlighten us."

"This Meathian would not leave our kingdom without a significant reason. Once she arrived and did not participate in daily palace life—"

"Such as?"

"Meals, cards, tea. She kept to her rooms almost every minute of her time here. She was late to her own presentation on the royal balcony." He paused and stepped closer to the king. "It was a direct insult to this kingdom, to the royal family, and to yourself, Your Majesty."

The king gestured toward the antechamber. "Prince Stephen, will you please join us?"

As Stephen stepped out of the room, the Lord Chamberlain paled considerably. Stephen walked onto the platform and stood next to his father. The knights quietly formed an arc behind the Lord Chamberlain, effectively separating him from the crowd of fairies filling the room. Several knights took positions around the king and Stephen. The Lord Chamberlain appeared like a trapped animal as he noticed the knights.

"Would you repeat your charges against Prince Stephen's intended, now that he stands before you?"

The Lord Chamberlain looked at the knights behind him again. "I may have overstated things."

Stephen stepped forward. "Was the princess advised of the expectations and the household schedule?"

"I—I—"

"Was she provided with a secretary?"

The Lord Chamberlain remained silent.

Stephen took another step forward. It was difficult to keep his hands at his sides instead of strangling the man as he had strangled Morgen. "Did you provide her with meals? A lady's maid? The very basics, such as a fire to keep her warm?" He curled his hands into tight fists as the atrocities waged against Morgen hit him again. "Did you take any steps to welcome her into the royal household and extend the privileges that befit a princess?"

When the Lord Chamberlain remained silent, Stephen descended the steps from the throne platform.

"You did not. You presented the worst of our kingdom. You, sir, are worse than the depiction you so arrogantly displayed of the Meathians. You left her to starve in a cold room. You tried to kill her." The crowd behind the knights gasped again. "You are the worst kind of fairy. You are evil." He turned to face the king. "He colluded with the Red Caps."

The king sprung up from his throne and advanced to stand beside Stephen. "You called our enemy into our kingdom? You allowed them through our borders?"

The Lord Chamberlain backed up until he came up against the solid form of a knight. He flinched at the contact and looked from the king to the knight and back again. Stephen enjoyed his discomfort. "Sire, it was only to remove the Meathian from our kingdom."

"I do not care why you did it. You have committed treason."

"No, Sire, not treason. No."

"Take him."

Two knights took hold of the Lord Chamberlains arms.

"No, Sire! No!"

The king motioned to the knights and they half-walked and half-dragged the protesting man from the throne room.

Chapter Ten

"It is done."

Morgen looked up from her place on the settee in her sitting room as Stephen made the proclamation. He was flanked by knights as he approached her.

She stood. "The king is safe?"

He nodded. "And the former Lord Chamberlain is being shown to his new accommodations as we speak."

She drew in a breath. "What will happen to him?" In Meath, he would face significant pain in the dungeons as his punishment was meted to him.

Stephen drew near and gestured to the settee next to her.

Morgen smiled at the implied request to be near her. As he sat down, the knights took positions nearby.

She looked at them and grinned at the prince. "I feel very safe."

He took her hand in his and held it snugly between them. "I hope that is feeling to which you will become accustomed. My bride should not fear anything."

She sucked in a quick breath and asked the question that burned deep inside her. "Am I still your intended?"

"Of course." His brow furrowed. "Why would that change?"

"There has been a lot of trouble in the kingdom because of me."

"You merely brought to light things we needed to know."

"But the Lord Chamberlain—"

"Former Lord Chamberlain."

She nodded with a small smile. "The former Lord Chamberlain was a trusted advisor within the palace. The king depended upon him—"

"He abused his position. We cannot have such ideas within our borders."

"But—"

"You cannot take responsibility for his actions."

"What will happen to him?"

He tightened his grip on her hand. "Do you care?"

"He will suffer because of me."

"You did not cause him to attack you or attempt to subvert the king's authority." He loosened his hold as he leaned even closer. Morgen gasped as she swirled into the depths of his eyes. "Come with me."

Her cloak wrapped around her and Stephen ensured the clasp was secure. His hand slid down the length of her arm and wrapped around her hand as he led her out to the balcony.

"Fly with me."

Without questions, she lifted into the air by his side. Knights rose with them at a discreet distance as they flew across the fountain and the lake behind the palace. Morgen smiled when she realized they were headed toward the bridge over the babbling brook. After they touched down on the spongy ground, Morgen placed her hands on his arm and turned her face up to look at him. "This is my favorite place."

"Mine, too." He reached out to stroke her cheek. "Come." Stephen led her onto the bridge and together they watched the water dance across the rocks and disappear under the bridge. When he looked at her instead of the water, she turned to him. He lifted her left hand and touched the glittering diamond ring. "When I gave you this, I did not know you. I believed the rumors."

"What were those?"

He shook his head. "That is unimportant. I know you now and I love you."

Her heart swelled. "I love you, too."

The prince dropped to one knee and looked up at her. Tears filled her eyes. "Princess Fruhlingsmorgen, please agree to marry me. Not for the alliance or for our kingdoms, but for us. I promise you a life filled with all my love and all the protection within my abilities. I cannot promise never to make you angry, but I promise to stand by your side forever more."

She pulled him to his feet and clasped his hands to her chest. "I will marry you, my prince, my love."

He leaned closer and touched his lips to hers. Gentle frissons of lightning blazed through her. "I will make you a proper wife."

Stephen chuckled lightly. "Never that, my love, never that."

Epilogue

It was a perfect late June morning when Prince Stephen made his way down to the dungeons. As he descended the worn, damp steps into the dank maze of cells, Stephen was glad to hear the dripping of water and smell the odor of decay and wet stone. The former Lord Chamberlain deserved to live in this discomfort.

Stephen nodded to the guards he passed at regular intervals and finally stepped in front of the cell that held the traitor. The man's fine clothing had not fared well these past several months. As he turned to face the prince, Stephen could see the threads fraying where Morgan had cut his sleeve with the dagger. The hem of his frock coat was also tattered and he could see shiny and threadbare patches at the elbows and knees.

"Good morning, Your Royal Highness." The former Lord Chamberlain bowed and showed the shiny pate of his head.

Stephen did not answer him. Instead, he watched the man in silence.

"You look well, Your Royal Highness."

He cocked an eyebrow. "Do I?"

"Yes, sir."

"So, you approve of my wedding clothes?"

The man paled, which pleased Stephen more than he anticipated.

"You did not know that I am marrying my princess today?"

He managed only to shake his head.

"Yes." Stephen smiled and turned to allow the former Lord Chamberlain to view his formal wedding clothes. "This is the day Princess Morgen becomes the future queen of Carlow."

The prisoner's mouth gaped open and closed like a fish as he tried to make a sound.

"Despite all your machinations and treasonous acts, the girl you tried to discredit will become my wife. When the time comes, we will ascend the throne as king and queen. We will have children. From that day forward, every generation of the Carlowian royal family will bear the blood of Meath."

The man hissed and his eyes narrowed. Stephen was glad for the force field that separated himself from the angry man. He smiled at his discomfort.

"Every devious and underhanded thing you did to the princess, every traitorous act, has amounted only to your own incarceration. The princess will be my wife." Stephen turned away to leave the dungeons, but faced the prisoner again. "I was wrong. There was something more that was caused by your actions." He paused to make sure he had the former Lord Chamberlain's full attention. "It is because of you that I am completely in love with Princess Morgen. If it were not for the kidnapping you orchestrated, we would have likely remained strangers for a long time. Now, thanks to you, we are a love match." Stephen enjoyed the increased rage in the man's eyes. "I hope you think of that every minute you spend in these dungeons, which will be a lifetime based upon the king's ruling." He turned and then looked back at him. "A sentence I will uphold."

Stephen smiled broadly as he retraced his steps out of the dungeon and into the fresh air.

Morgen stared at her reflection in the full-length mirror as Lily closed the seam of her bridal gown. The silk-satin fabric glowed in the light that poured through the windows, offset by the soft white of the applique lace that covered the bottom half of the voluminous skirt. Handmade netting and lace accented the bottom edges of the three-quarter length sleeves and tickled her arms. It also edged the scooped neckline that set off her neck and shoulders. Morgen grinned as Lily fitted the matching belt around her waist. Tiny diamonds dotting the belt sparkled and caught her eye. She tucked in a small nosegay of orange blossoms and rosemary into the belt once it was secured in place.

"Those smell gorgeous."

Morgen smiled at Violet Moore, the stunning Lady of the Harvest. She had met the raven-haired beauty at a royal function and they had become fast friends. She fluffed the satin ribbon that was looped through the nosegay as Lady Fern brought the matching circlet to her side. It was settled onto her head and Violet and Lily anchored a featherlight veil to the back. The sheer veil flowed to the floor and spilled over the modest train of her skirts. The veil touched her skin like butterfly wings and cocooned her in its draping folds.

Lady Fern stepped before her. "You are beautiful."

Violet adjusted the circlet a smidge. "I agree. You are a dream."

Morgen's cheeks heated as she looked at Violet and Lady Fern. "I am so glad you will be there with me." She smiled at the thought of being attended by these two fairies. "I never thought I would find such wonderful friends." She turned to Lily. "You have added immensely to my wedding day. I am so happy to have you here."

The little fairy blushed as she fussed with Morgen's gown. "Thank you, Your Royal Highness."

A knock sounded at the door. Lily opened it a crack, murmured, and closed it again with the palm of her hand against the line where the edge of the door matched the length of the wall. She turned around and leaned against the door. "They are ready for you."

Morgen's heart hammered in her chest as she glanced at her reflection one last time before following The Gilded and The Lady of the Harvest into the corridor. Footmen lined the walls and bowed to her as she passed. Somehow, she managed the staircase without tumbling to the lower floors and went outside to stand under the same portico she entered when she had first arrived in Revlin. That was when she thought the Lord Chamberlain was her ally. She drew in a sharp breath at the memory of his betrayal and the pain inflicted by the Red Caps. Her ankle throbbed where her largest scar lay and she touched the almost-invisible scar at her temple.

"You are beautiful."

She turned to Lady Fern at her ping.

"Your scar is a part of who you are and does not detract."

Morgen nodded and watched as Lady Fern and Miss Violet, her two bridesmaids, stepped into an ornate carriage decorated with swags of roses and ribbons in her signature color. As they moved off with the jangle of harnesses and the creak of the large wooden wheels, another carriage took its place. This carriage was enclosed, but made of large panes of crystal. Diamonds dripped from the finials at the corners of the roof, and more roses and ribbon swayed with the carriage's movement. Finely-dressed footmen stood on their platforms at the rear of the carriage and the driver at up front with his second.

"Your Royal Highness." Another footman opened the carriage door for her and stood holding the handle.

Morgen walked down the sky-blue carpet to the carriage and allowed the footman to assist her inside. He lifted her voluminous skirts into the carriage and she settled the folds around her. She brought the veil around and allowed it to float down onto her lap and the front of her skirts, as instructed by Mrs. Henson, the dressmaker.

As they drove out of the palace grounds, a deafening cheer filled the air. Morgen swallowed her nerves, wishing she had a companion in the carriage with her, and waved to the undulating masses that lined the road. Every time she waved, the crowds cheered louder and she couldn't help but smile. Since her arrival, these fairies had welcomed her into their hearts. They deserved all her attention and love. With a smile, she continued to wave to both sides of the carriage as she made her way through the city to the large cathedral. The volume of the clanging bells increased as she approached. Finally, the carriage came to a stop and Lady Fern and Violet stepped forward as a footman opened her door.

When her shoe touched the wide blue carpet that led up into the impressive building, the crowd's volume increased. She could feel the tugging of her bridesmaids as they straightened the folds of her skirts and arranged the length of her veil. At the top of the stairs, she turned and waved to the crowd, which waved and cheered in return. Infused with the warmth of the kingdom's love, she turned to walk into the depths of the cathedral to marry the man of her heart.

The End

Turn the page for a preview of

Book 3

Of

The Fairies of Carlow:

The

Commoner

Available now exclusively on Amazon

Chapter One

"When will it end?"

Her Royal Highness Princess Cecilia glanced over her shoulder at the knights escorting her through the royal grounds of the palace. Situated near the center of the capital city of Revlin, the palace was the home of the royal family of Carlow—her home. These days it was more a gilded cage than a regal family home. Her parents, King Rork and Queen Claire, had severely restricted what she could do. Cecilia sighed and shifted in her saddle. Ever since the wretched Red Caps had kidnapped Princess Morgen last year and nearly tortured her elder brother's intended to death, she hadn't been able be outdoors without a full cadre of knights—even to tour the royal grounds around the castle. She was used to exploring the beautiful grounds and thick forest on horseback or on foot without a guard. They had been required only when she traveled outside the ornate fence that separated the palace from the city. Cecilia reached down and patted her mare's neck.

"You would like to be on a less rigid routine, as well, would you not?"

The horse tossed its head and nickered in response. BRC, Before Red Caps, she rode this beautiful white and gray mare alone across the wide and open lawns of the royal landscape, and through the trees to the sparkling creek. She had explored the ornate gardens and the decorative knots of herbs and plants on foot. Cecilia glanced at the armed guards that surrounded her and bit her lower lip. All that was changed now. Even after the Red Caps had grabbed Her Exalted Highness Lady Fern the Gilded and dragged her away from Carlow and into Red Caps land, she hadn't been under this much protection. The only request from her parents had been to stay away from the border. After all, that is where Lady Fern was walking when the Caps reached through the Carlowian force field to grab her. Cecilia shivered at the thought. She couldn't imagine what Lady Fern, and her new sister-in-law, Princess Morgen, had endured at the hands of those wicked creatures with their hats soaked with the bright red blood of their enemies. She hoped she would act as bravely as they had but suspected she would fall far short. She knew she lacked the courage and wits needed to survive such an ordeal. With a soft nudge from her heels, her horse accelerated into a canter.

"Your Royal Highness, please slow your mount. We have not cleared the forest ahead of you deep enough for that rate of speed."

"Sorry, Smoke." She patted her horse's neck again. "It is back to a sedate walk for the both of us."

Reluctantly she slowed, and the knights tightened their grouping around her. She sighed again, despite her mother's admonishments that it was an unladylike habit. Plodding along was a boring way to tour the grounds, but it was the only way she was able to leave the palace walls. Every week this dull ride afforded her a few hours in the fresh air. Otherwise she was stuck inside. Cecilia shook her head at her train of thought.

Poor, pitiful me. I must remain inside a cozy palace filled with books, art, and all the help I need.

She rolled her eyes and allowed Smoke to grab a mouthful of tender Spring grass. The knights tightened their circle even closer as two other knights rode out of the forest and cantered to the group.

"The way is clear, Sir."

The lead knight, Sir Caleb, looked at her. "You may

proceed."

She nodded and clucked to Smoke. The mare obediently started forward and Cecilia watched the sunlight dim as the air turned cooler. She followed the path deeper into the forest and soon could hear the creek as water burbled around boulders.

"Will you be stopping at the bridge?"

"Not today." She wouldn't be able to enjoy leaning over the wood rail and watching the current carry sticks into the distance.

"Pardon, Your Royal Highness, but are you well?"

She looked at the young knight who rode beside her and grimaced. "I apologize, Sir Thomas. I am feeling a bit under the weather today."

"Shall we return to the palace?"

She shrugged and ran her fingers through Smoke's mane. The knight remained quiet. Cecilia looked at him from under her lashes and saw only patience in his features. Her heart went out to these knights, who were highly trained and ended up escorting her through the most protected land in the kingdom. Sir Thomas, in particular, had been a knight for only a short time. He had been elevated after meritorious service to the crown. "I am sorry that you are attached to such a boring detail."

"It isn't, is not, boring to protect you, Your Highness."

She smiled at his use of a contraction, which was not allowed of the royals or nobility. Sometimes his country fairy roots came through. She remembered the way her father had called Thomas to the royal balcony after the Battle of Carlow. The young man had been so nervous, but his blush had deepened and included his ears when the king proclaimed he was thereafter to be known as Sir Thomas. Cecilia couldn't help but smile at the memory. He had been a hero during the battle and it was gratifying to see him so well-rewarded.

"Your Royal Highness, shall we return to the palace?"

She looked up at Sir Matthew, the older knight who seemed to take her safety as his personal mission. He remained quiet, waiting for her answer.

"Yes."

As a group, they turned away from the creek and plodded back down the path toward the castle. She bit back another sigh at the sheer tedium of the ride. How she longed to feel the wind in her hair, to hear the snap of her skirts as Smoke galloped through the fields! She wanted to feel the exhilaration of a good ride, with the danger of jumping rail fences and forging water. BRC, she had given her maid apoplectic fits over the state of her skirts after such rides, spattered as they were with mud and water. These days, all she risked was a fine film of dust thrown up from the hooves of all her escorts.

Finally, they arrived at the stables and she fed Smoke a carrot before leaving her in the capable hands of a groomsman. The knights walked with her through the rose garden and toward the palace. In a fit of defiance, Cecilia stretched her wings and flew into the air. It felt so good to give her wings a workout, as if stretching a cramped limb. She continued to fly far above the palace, wishing she could go out over the capitol city of Revlin and swoop amongst the trees. She might even go to the shore of the lake and listen to the gentle lap of waves.

As she flew higher and higher, she refused to acknowledge the pings of the knights who immediately followed her into the air. It was only when an image of Sir Caleb flashed in her mind that she acquiesced. Reluctantly, she allowed the knight to enter her mind.

"Your Royal Highness, please descend and withdraw into the palace." His voice was laced with repressed anger.

Above her, the golden hue of the protective dome that surrounded the palace was very near. It wouldn't take much to follow her dreams and cross the threshold into Revlin. But, then what? All that would happen was disgrace at her disobedience. It wasn't worth it. Obediently, she lowered herself to the balcony outside her suite of rooms and alit on the stone floor.

"Thank you, Your Royal Highness."

She severed the link and immediately regretted not giving an answer to the knight. He was only doing his duty. She vowed to apologize the next time she saw him. With a light tap of her wand, which she had withdrawn from the pocket of air at her side, the doors were unlocked, and she walked inside her sitting room. Warm air surrounded her as a blaze crackled merrily in the fireplace.

"Home again." She turned in a slow circle and took in the all-too-familiar painted walls and plush furnishings. Her anger at her velvet shackles had disappeared, and all that was left was a profound feeling of sadness. "I cannot take this much longer."

She pulled out the long hatpin that held her tightly-woven straw riding hat in place and tossed it toward a plush chair near the fireplace. The long, curled ostrich feathers that adorned the crown of the hat riffled in the air and the satin ribbon fluttered as the ends trailed behind. The hat landed on the cushioned and tufted armchair with a soft thud. Cecilia stared at it for a moment before tossing the hat pin onto the chair as well. She returned to the doors leading to her balcony, threw them open and breathed in the scented gentle breeze. Clouds scudded across the sky, dropping the temperature and bringing the threat of rain. She drew in another deep breath and the scented breeze wafted in through the windows, making the blush-colored silk curtains flutter and billow. Another sigh escaped her as the sky darkened and the clouds grew more ominous.

She closed the doors and leaned one shoulder against the window frame. It would be so nice to live her life as it had been BRC, with fewer restrictions and more say in her life. Cecilia plucked at the white undersleeve that showed through the slashes in the middle of her light pink sleeves as her mind argued with her emotions. The Red Caps are dangerous! Look at what they did to Princess Morgen and Lady Fern. And they were certainly protected. After all, Princess Morgen was her brother's intended and under the care of the palace. Lady Fern was a Gilded, one of the most illustrious fairies in the land. And her father was the nephew of the king and a member of the border council. Still, the Red Caps were able to cross the border into Carlow and kidnap them.

Okay, so there was some basis for the actions of the palace. The Great Battle with the Red Caps had been one thing, but once Princess Morgen was kidnapped the restrictions had avalanched upon her. Thankfully, the beautiful princess had been rescued and was now happily married to Prince Stephen. They were blissfully happy. She stared sightlessly into the distance. She wanted to be happy, too. How she longed to go beyond the palace walls and be away from the watchful eyes that constantly surrounded her.

"I must get away from all this. She crossed to the fireplace to warm herself and rested an arm on the mantle. "I must find some time for myself—outside."

But how? It was impossible to escape her escorts during a

ride. The knights were extremely capable and would catch her in a moment. And, they would know the instant that she flew through the protective dome over the palace if she tried to leave without consent. Sometimes it took all her strength not to scream. In frustration. In anger. She curled her hands into fists and turned away from the fireplace. She allowed herself to flop down on the settee, despite the rigorous training of her governess. It was only in these rooms that she could get away with such slovenly behavior.

She really didn't mind. Sometimes it was difficult to maintain the perfect seated and standing posture that her position required, but it wasn't a new restriction. It was the ladylike thing to do. She drew in a breath and tried to kick off her riding boots, but they held firm. Molded to her feet and made of the softest leather, the boots were impossible to doff without assistance, just like her gowns. Cecilia stopped trying to kick them off and conjured some tea. A tray appeared where she had swept her hand, laden with a delicate porcelain tea pot covered with tiny rosebuds and a matching plate that held a few cookies. She poured the hot tea into a matching cup and took a sip. The simplicity of the snack made her smile. It was perfect.

She wasn't through her first cup of tea when a knock sounded at her door. Immediately after, her lady's maid, Snap, entered the suite.

"It is time to prepare for the evening meal, Your Royal Highness."

Cecilia nodded and set her cup on the tray before waving her hand to disappear the tea things into a wisp of smoke. Once in her bedroom, she sat on a tufted chair by the windows as Snap tugged off her boots. With a deft application of her wand tip to the back seam, the dark-haired fairy undid Cecilia's gown and twirled it up over her head. Standing in her chemise and stockings, Cecilia kept her arms raised overhead as a silk gown was flown out of the armoire and floated down over her. Lowering her arms, Cecilia waited as Snap applied the tip of her wand to the seam to close the fabric. Once in her slippers, she sat at her dressing table and her hair was brushed and twisted into a graceful chignon.

"Lovely."

She caught Snap's eye in the mirror. "Thank you."

The young fairy curtseyed. "I will take care of your riding things while you are at the family table." She flicked her wand at the gown and boots to miniaturize them and floated them into her hand. "Enjoy your evening." She curtseyed again and silently left the bedroom, carrying her small burden. Cecilia heard the main door to her suite click shut and scrutinized herself in the mirror. Snap always knew how to help her look her best. She smoothed a few runaway strands of hair and spritzed on a bit of perfume. The light scent of roses mixed with an earthiness that reminded her of rain. The mantle clock chimed the hour.

Cecilia glanced at it in alarm. "Oh, shoot, I am late."

In a flurry of silks and ribbons, she rushed through her suite, slowing only when she opened the door to the corridor. As sedately as possible, she made her way to the family dining room. It wouldn't do to be seen scurrying through the palace like a mouse.

Only slightly out of breath, she arrived and waited for the footman to open the door.

"My dear, you look lovely."

Cecilia smiled at her mother, Queen Claire, as she crossed the thickly-carpeted room. "Thank you." She sat on the curvy sofa beside her mother and waited for the remaining stragglers from her family. Once Prince Rupert arrived (wasn't she pleased not to be the last one!), the family walked into the dining room.

A footman pulled out her chair and she sat at the table with the rest of her boisterous family. Conversations filled the air and laughter often punctuated their words. Prince Rupert sat next to her; Prince Stephen, the crowned prince and heir to the throne, sat at her father's left; and Princess Morgen sat at his right. Cecilia's gaze lingered on her. She was radiant as her stomach swelled with the first royal grandchild. A smile played on her lips as she watched Stephen, her dauntless brother who have proven himself courageous in battle, do everything he could for his wife. He was completely under her power. In fact, he could not do enough for her, eager to smooth her day and prevent her from exerting herself. He would probably cut his wife's meat if she would let him. Cecilia giggled at the scene in her imagination and shook her head. Her grin caught the attention of her mother, seated a few chairs down at the foot of the table.

Queen Claire smiled in return. "Will you not share your happiness, my dear?"

Cecilia chewed her bottom lip for a moment as she considered her mother's request. She couldn't tell her family of the comical view she had of her brother and sister-in-law. That would be too humiliating for both Stephen and Morgen. She couldn't be unkind to them. Instead, she seized the opportunity to discuss the issue that had been bothering her for so long. With a deep breath to bolster her courage, she took the plunge.

"I was remembering before."

"Before what?"

"Before—" She tipped her head toward Morgen. Her sister-in-law paled and placed her hands protectively on her abdomen. Stephen reached over and stroked his wife's arm.

"Not you, Morgen, but what happened to you." Cecilia was gratified with Morgen's small nod of understanding. Cecilia cleared her throat as she glanced at her mother and father. "Well, what happened—it changed things." She looked back at Morgen and Stephen before returning her attention to her parents again. "For everyone."

"For you."

"Well, yes." She looked away from her father's penetrating

236

gaze and down at her fingers, laced in her lap. "I understand why I was restricted to the palace grounds, but when will it end?" She looked at Stephen. "I do not want anything more to happen to Morgen—" She looked at all the faces around the table—faces she loved. "Not to anyone." She sighed. "But I feel that I must be allowed to be myself, to have my freedom returned. I must be allowed to fend for myself." She gave her mother a small smile. "Just a little."

The queen compressed her lips. Cecilia turned to look at her father. He shook his head slightly. "It has been only a year since—what happened to our new daughter. We must continue to be vigilant, to protect those who are in the most danger."

"How am I in danger?"

His eyes narrowed. He was unused to anyone, let alone his daughter, questioning his edicts. "You are in danger because of your high birth. You must understand this."

"You do not want to be taken, do you?" Stephen's words sounded harsh.

She glared at him. "Things have changed since Morgen—" She looked the ravishing princess. "I am sorry. This must be painful for you." When Morgen shook her head and smiled, Cecilia returned her attention to Stephen and continued. "Things are different since she was taken. Are our borders not stronger?" She looked again at her father. "Are we not more secure?"

"To be sure."

"Then why must I be constantly escorted? Why can I not be alone? It is stifling." "Cecilia, do not be stupid."

She glared at her twin brother. "Keep to yourself, Rupert."

He narrowed his eyes at her and she expected him to stick his tongue out, as he had when they were younger.

"Rupert. Cecilia."

The quiet warning from her mother stopped Cecilia from flinging a retort at her brother. Instead, she clenched her hands together in her lap and continued to chew her bottom lip.

"This is the end of this conversation." She looked at her father and knew by the determined set of his jaw that it would do little good to continue. Her father, her parents, would not be swayed. She picked up her fork and allowed the tines to beat out a tune on the table, in direct opposition to the table manners that had so patiently been taught to her.

Once the footmen served the first course, her fork was better employed. Yet, the meal seemed interminable as she chafed with the results of her discussion with her parents. Finally, the last course was finished. Instead of following her mother and sister-in-law into the parlor for tea, Cecilia begged off. She could see that her mother didn't believe she had a headache, but it was the best excuse she could come up with at the time.

Once in her suite, Cecilia curled up in a chair near her fireplace. The heat of the flames did little to warm her as she stewed about her father's refusal to ease the restrictions settled on her since the last Red Caps infiltration. She let out a huff of air and stared into the wavering flames. Something must change. Cecilia stood up and paced the length of her room. She needed to figure out a way to accept the limitations placed on her or at least force a change.

Throughout her life, she had been taught to take a stand for her beliefs. Now, it was time to act on those lessons despite the defiance it would levy toward her parents. In a fit of pique, Cecilia opened her window and stepped out onto her balcony. If they wouldn't allow her to leave with their permission, she would leave without it. Now. Not giving the consequences of her actions another thought, she extended her wings and took to the air. As quickly as possible, she flew north and blasted through the force field surrounding the palace grounds. Ignoring the searing pain that coursed through her at the breach, she flew with determination. She knew the knights had been alerted of her flight as soon as she approached the field. They would be in pursuit faster than she wished.

Her breath came rapidly with the exertion of flying. The past year of restrictions had severely compromised her endurance. Unable to look over her shoulder to see if anyone was following her, Cecilia concentrated on staying aloft. It was difficult. The treetops were only gray shadows in the rainy night as clouds blocked light from the moon and stars. Gasping for air, she continued to fly north.

"Ouch!" The sharp needles of a tree grabbed at her ankles as she fought to maintain altitude. It was becoming more difficult and her wings felt as though they were filled with lead. Finally, she wasn't able to stay above the trees and wound her way through the trunks and branches. The trees seemed to jump out at her as she flew, barely avoiding a few as the stitch in her side bit at her.

When she couldn't move her wings another inch, Cecilia landed on the soft and damp ground. Knowing she couldn't risk taking a few minutes to catch her breath, she forced her slipper-clad feet to keep moving. The sodden skirts and petticoats of her gown tripped her up and she grabbed at the heavy yards of fabric to lift her skirts out of the way. As she rushed through the thick forest, she crossed many paths. Cecilia avoided taking their smoother, and easier, way, knowing she needed to stay away from any people or villages. It wouldn't do to run away from the palace, only to be turned in by a well-meaning subject of the crown.

She didn't know how far she was from the capitol city of Revlin or if she managed to continue north. She didn't know why she was so determined to move north, except for the fact that the bulk of the kingdom of Carlow lay in that direction. She would run into the border if she went any other direction. The Red Caps lay directly south of Revlin and other, friendlier, kingdoms lay to the east and west. No matter how she felt about the new rules, she certainly wasn't prepared to cross the border. That would be the height of idiocy, not to mention painful. Crossing the border without permission was a hundred times more excruciating than crossing the force field over the palace, if it could be crossed at all. She couldn't imagine that level of pain. Breaching the border had been painful enough!

Finally, unable to take another step and gasping for a lungful of air, Cecilia leaned against the rough trunk of a pine tree and rested until her wheezing ended. A noise captured her attention. Holding her breath, she listened for the distinct whir of wings that would indicate the knights had found her, but all that met her ears were the sounds of the forest. She sighed in relief and focused her attention on the murmur of wind blowing through the branches as she continued to slow her breathing.

"I must keep moving." Her whispered words were as loud as a shout in the darkness.

Ignoring a deep desire to remain where she was, Cecilia continued to run through the forest. Rain pelted her face and shadow shrouded the forest in a dark blanket. She wished she could see better, to be able to pick a clear path through the trees, but knew the lack of moonlight helped to conceal her. Her toes and the soles of her feet pricked with pain as she stumbled over roots and rocks. Cecilia racked her brain as she tried to remember the lessons in navigation that had been so uncomplainingly taught by her tutor but couldn't recall how to determine direction without any light. She needed the stars, or at least the moon to help her continue north. Hopefully, she wasn't running in a circle and accidentally returning to Revlin.

Small hollows and dips in the forest floor jarred her and sent her to her knees as she continued to run. Something caught her foot and sent her sprawling, the heels of her hands gauging into the damp dirt. Small shards of pain pierced her hands.

"That is it." She scrambled to her feet and brushed the dirt from her palms. Her knees were sore and, she imagined, bloody. In a few minutes, she came upon a narrow deer path and threw caution to the wind. Choosing her direction at random, she walked down the smoother dirt, risking exposure for the sake of staying on her feet. The opportunity to escape further pain from falling was worth the risk of exposure. As she continued down the path, the rain clouds parted slightly and allowed a small shaft of feeble moonlight through to illuminate the landscape around her. Instead, she used the light to scrutinize the palms of her hands and saw dark streaks that she imagined were dried blood. Patting them lightly on her damp skirts, she increased her speed to a jog, ignoring the pain caused by the rapid pace.

After only a short distance, she gripped her side and leaned against a tree. "Ow." She breathed in through her nose and let out a most unladylike gush of air. Bending to the side, she rubbed the pain, trying to ease its grip. The snap of a twig caught her attention and her heart rate shot up. The knights had found her!

Without another thought, she ran through the forest, keeping parallel to the narrow path in order to follow its contours while remaining as hidden as possible. No other snapping twig sounds caught her attention as she gasped her way through the trees. Cecilia slowed down and alternated between jogging and walking until she caught her breath and her energy levels increased. With concerted effort, she quickened into a run and darted out onto the path.

"Hey!"

Cecilia turned at the voice and saw the hulking shape of a horse just before her. With a cry she flung up her arm as a sharp pain cut into her head. The darkness of night enveloped her, and a thick layer of pine needles and soft dirt cushioned her fall.

Made in the USA
Las Vegas, NV
11 December 2020